MW01128847

When Harry Met Rose

Mr Selfridge and the Search for Love

Maria Malone

Copyright © 2015 Maria Malone
All rights reserved.

Cover design: Emma King, The Curved House
Formatting Polgarus Studio

For Peggy and John

1.

The day everything changed, in May, 1890, Harry Selfridge was in his office enjoying a rare moment of peace. He paced about, his mind sifting and sorting ideas, now and then pausing to jot something down. Ideas were the thing, the means by which a good business became great. Arguably, Marshall Field was Chicago's finest store but, in Harry's view, there was always room for improvement. Ever-vigilant, he was constantly on the lookout for ways to drum up more business and at the same time make the experience of shopping more enjoyable; less of a chore, more an event.

He crossed to the window. Below, State Street bustled. Out front, carriages waited in line while, inside, wealthy customers shopped. The store occupied the best location in the city and Harry had made sure to bag the best office. Marshall Field, whose enterprise it was, seemed content with a dingy room as his workplace but Harry had worked hard to get where he was and wanted an office that reflected his efforts. Since he held most of his meetings there and important customers had a tendency to drop in on him, his surroundings had to be suitable. It was vital to make the right impression. As he stood at the window, hands clasped behind his back, taking in the view, his mind remained on the business of the store. His latest venture, the opening of a restaurant, had proved an immediate success – beyond his expectations. It seemed the women who shopped at Marshall Field found it convenient to stop for coffee or tea, or punctuate their browsing with lunch. The atmosphere was right, he was certain of that, and his idea to place an American Beauty rose on each table had been enthusiastically received. Although pleased enough with the way the place had caught on he couldn't help feeling he had perhaps been too modest in terms of its scale. In business, it didn't pay to think small and he sensed he was missing an opportunity; that there was room for a much bigger enterprise.

Harry Selfridge was in the habit of visiting every one of the store's departments each day without fail. The hour he chose to tour the floor, and the route he followed, varied, so that the staff, never sure when he would show up, were more likely to remain alert at all times.

On that particular day, Harry had been on the shop floor in the morning and found trade to be brisk. Strolling from one department to another, he made a point of exchanging a few words with both customers and staff, going out of his way to make everyone who came through the store's elegant doors – from those shopping for bargains in the basement to the high-society, high-spending, women frequenting the fashion department – know that their business was valued. Marshall Field had a first-rate reputation for service and Harry was always looking to raise the already high standards.

He checked his pocket watch. An hour until his next meeting. Time enough to get along to the restaurant and have coffee. He took a fresh shirt from those hanging in the cupboard in the corner of the office and changed, taking a fragrant gardenia from the vase on the side table and placing it in the buttonhole of his suit jacket. Letting his secretary know where he would be, he made his way to the restaurant.

Every table was occupied. A good sign. From his vantage position just inside the entrance Harry's gaze swept the room and settled on the table in the furthest corner where a lone woman sat. He recognized Rosalie Buckingham, a former debutante fast becoming influential in Chicago as a property developer. Miss Buckingham had been in the store before and once or twice she and Harry had been at the same social occasion but their paths had never quite collided. He wondered if this was the moment to introduce himself, yet she seemed so deep in thought he was loath to intrude. Something about her struck him, not that he could have put into words quite what it was. It was as if she was in her own secret world. As he watched, she reached for the rose from the vase on the table and inhaled its scent. Harry felt an odd flicker of something he would later identify as longing and in that moment, Rosalie, a woman he had not yet even spoken to, found her way under his skin.

It had been a while since Rosalie Buckingham set aside time to relax away from the pressures of business. For the best part of a year she had been toiling long hours, doing little but work. Or so it seemed. Relaxation had been low down on her list of priorities. Not that there had been much choice in the matter. If she was to make a success of the business she now ran in partnership with her brother-in-law, Frank, a good deal of time and effort was called for. The pair of them made an impressive team, both equally hard-working and with a shared determination to make a success of things. All the same, it was in nobody's interest to work to the point of exhaustion and she had felt herself coming dangerously close in recent weeks. Her sister, Anna, had insisted she have a day to herself, to ease the load, as she put it, and Frank had agreed. She would be no use to anyone if she overdid things. She smiled. So unused was she to having any free time, let alone a whole day, she had not known what to do with herself. Shopping at Marshall Field had been a spur of the moment decision. A good one, it seemed. How long was it since she browsed Chicago's best department store at her leisure? Too long, she concluded.

Her mind wandered to the houses now being built on land at Hyde Park on the outskirts of the city. What had begun as a dream – somewhat a pipedream, if she was honest – was fast becoming a reality. Several elegant villas on the Harper Lane site were now complete. The spacious properties each had an expansive front yard and a driveway leading to a courtyard with stables at the back, since the kind of well-off people wanting a property a little way out of the city would invariably have a carriage with one or two horses.

The next phase of the development, the building of what Rosalie described as artists' cottages, would soon be underway. In recent months she had wondered if her vision for so many houses on such a scale might be too ambitious but now that the properties were going up – and proving popular – her initial doubts were receding. The uncertainty and sleepless nights that had accompanied the project were, she believed, a price worth paying.

In the restaurant, soft golden light from the ornate chandelier in the centre of the room made the panelled walls gleam and lent an air of intimacy to the surroundings. The space was small, yet sumptuous, exactly as it had been described to her. She took off her gloves and set them aside on the damask cloth. Around her was the sound of silverware against fine china, the voices of other diners. A waiter in a white jacket with gold trim placed a pot of tea on the table and asked if there was anything else he could bring for her. She shook her head and the upright young man gave a deferential bow. Her sister had been right to enthuse about the standard of service in the newly-opened restaurant. It was excellent. Small touches, indicating that someone had given the venture a great deal of thought, caught her eye; napkins edged in lace, embellished with the name of the store and, along the walls in ornate gilt frames, fashionable paintings in the style that had become known as Impressionist. She knew about art and, by the look of it, the pictures were originals. The one nearest to her, a sunset in yellows and orange, was exquisite. In the centre of her table was a rose, an extravagant pinkish-red bloom. Glancing around, she saw that each table had one and could not resist plucking the flower from its crystal vase and breathing in the fragrance. For a moment, she closed her eyes. If only she could find a scent just like it she would wear it all the time. The thought made her smile again. The waiter was back, pouring tea into a delicate cup decorated with the same kind of splashy rose as the one in her hand. The distinctive smoky scent of Lapsang Souchong reached her nostrils. Replacing the rose in its vase it came to her to speak to the landscape team about planting similar expansive blooms in the open spaces surrounding Harper Lane. Her gaze turned again to the paintings as she gave her tea a moment to cool. Originals, most certainly. Rosalie Buckingham, entirely at home in her surroundings, sipped her tea with no sense of being observed.

'Excuse me for interrupting, I don't mean to impose if you're waiting for someone …' Rosalie turned to find Harry Selfridge standing beside her table. She had been so caught up in her thoughts she had not even been aware of his approach.

He gave an uncertain smile. 'I was wondering if I might join you.'

Although they had never been formally introduced, Rosalie had seen Harry Selfridge at various social occasions and found him intriguing. He had presence, a powerful energy, which together constituted that rare thing, charisma. Well-known in Chicago for his sharp business brain and flamboyant style, Harry Selfridge with his well-cut clothes and colourful silk ties represented the very opposite of the dour, restrained Marshall Field. Given the stark differences of the two men it seemed all the more surprising that Harry had risen through the ranks with such speed to become so influential at the store. Rosalie knew he had to be outstanding at his job to have done so well.

She gestured at the seat opposite. 'Please, do sit down. I'm not expecting anyone.'

Harry hesitated. 'You seemed deep in thought. Really, I don't mean to intrude.'

She gave him a warm smile. 'I would be happy to have your company.'

'We've not actually met-' he began.

'-I know who you are,' she cut in. 'Everyone says you're the ideas man here.'

He gave a broad smile. 'I'm flattered.' He held out a hand. 'Harry Selfridge.'

'Rosalie Buckingham.'

He held onto Rosalie's hand a fraction longer than he had meant to until she slid it from his grasp. Afraid he had been clumsy, pushy, even, he looked away but when he looked up again she met his gaze, seemingly unfazed. The warmth of her smile was unambiguous. Her eyes, he noticed, were the colour of amber.

She took in the gardenia in the buttonhole, the subtle scent of cologne. 'You're famous in Chicago, Mr Selfridge,' she said. 'I must confess, it's a while since I was in the store and I've seen a lot of changes. I'm guessing that's your influence.'

'Please, call me Harry,' he said, and again immediately wondered if he had been too forward. 'I hope you like what you've seen so far.'

She glanced around the room. 'This, for instance, wasn't here the last time I came into the store – *Harry*.'

Harry. 'We only opened the restaurant a few weeks ago. It's proving very popular.'

'Was it one of your innovations?'

He waited a beat before answering, trying to work out whether she approved of what he'd done, all at once realizing how keen he was to impress her. 'Actually, it was. So far, from everything our customers have said, it's proving a real asset. They seem to like it very much.' When Rosalie said nothing, he went on. 'I'm always keen for all shades of opinion, however, even if it's to say we haven't quite got it right.'

'Oh, I'd say you've got it just right,' she said.

The white-jacketed waiter appeared with a silver pot of coffee and fresh tea.

'Can I bring you anything else, Mr Selfridge?'

Harry glanced at Rosalie. She shook her head.'

'No, that's all, thank you, Mr Francis,' Harry told the waiter.

An elderly woman accompanied by a younger female companion came over to speak to Harry and compliment what she termed the superb service in every department at Marshall Field. He got to his feet, addressing the woman by name, and thanking her. As he took his seat again he apologized to Rosalie for the interruption.

'I confess I had some doubts opening a restaurant would appeal to our more traditional customers but it seems they also like it,' he said

Rosalie looked about her. 'I was thinking, I might just have to steal one of your ideas.'

Harry gave her a curious look.

'I'm assuming it *was* your idea to place such a lovely rose on each of the tables.'

'You like it? For me, the American Beauty is one of the finest flowers there is.'

'I'm thinking maybe I could plant some over at Hyde Park. Now I've seen how wonderful they are. The scent is divine.' Harry knew about the Hyde Park development. It was attracting a lot of attention. 'As long as you wouldn't mind, of course,' she said. 'I wouldn't want to step on your toes.'

He gave a shake of the head. 'Not at all. I would be only too happy.'

They sat in comfortable silence for a few seconds.

Rosalie said, 'You know, I'm very curious about the paintings you have here – they look as if they're originals.'

'You're an art lover?'

'I paint – a little.' She nodded in the direction of the sunset that had caught her eye. 'Nothing like that, I'm afraid. The colours and the light – they really are quite extraordinary.'

'It's by Monet,' Harry said. It was about all he knew. Much as he enjoyed having the paintings around he had not yet come to appreciate precisely why people were getting so excited about the work of the artists dubbed Impressionists. Their pictures looked … well, a little on the simplistic side, if he was honest. Not that he was about to say so since from what Rosalie Buckingham had said and the rapt look on her face, she was quite a fan.

'It's wonderful you've brought great art into a department store,' she said. 'Really, when I came out today I had no idea a shopping trip would prove so uplifting.'

Harry's mind was racing. An exhibition of Monet's paintings was coming to the Chicago Art Institute. He had been in discussion with the curator about loaning some of the store's artworks, something he knew would create ample opportunity for extensive press coverage. He decided to jump right in.

'Miss Buckingham, Marshall Field has a connection with the upcoming Monet exhibition in the city. I would be honoured if you would be my guest at the gala opening.'

Rosalie held his gaze for what seemed like an age. 'Please, call me Rose.'

Rose. Harry beamed, already having decided that from that moment on he would forever associate the delightful Miss Buckingham with the flower he prized above all others – the American Beauty rose.

2.

Lois Selfridge knew at once that something special must have happened for Harry to come home from the store in such high spirits. He had bounded in, embraced her, and raced upstairs to freshen up and change for dinner. Lois had smiled at his almost-boyish enthusiasm. Her son had always been the same. His feelings, good or bad, were writ large in his face. As she relaxed in the drawing room of the home they shared in one of Chicago's best suburbs and waited for Harry to reappear and dispense whatever good news he had, she reflected on how much their lives had changed in the space of a few years. They had gone from scraping by, never having enough money, living on the edge of poverty, to wealth and privilege. Harry had done everything he could to create a better life for the two of them. It had been anything but plain sailing yet his spirit and determination had not once wavered. Lois had brought him up to believe in himself and follow his dreams. He had made her so proud.

It had almost always been just the two of them. Harry's father, Robert, had gone off to fight in the Civil War in 1861 when his youngest son was five years old, and had never returned. Harry's older brothers, Charles and Robert Junior had died in separate, tragic incidents. At times, Lois had felt close to going under but had always known in her heart that she would not. She had her youngest son to consider and there was nothing she would not do to give him the best chance in life.

A fire burned in the grate, sending sparks shooting up the chimney. In the hall, the mahogany grandfather clock gave a series of soft chimes. Lois thought about the opulence of her home with its fine furniture, the hand-painted wall coverings and heavy silk drapes. In front of her, on the mantelpiece was a porcelain figure Harry had brought back from one of his trips to Paris and beside it a line of miniature Chinese ceramics. They had cost a lot, she expected, although he was coy about how much he spent on such things. Fripperies, he called them, as though they were of no consequence, yet they both knew that the good things in life mattered; having come from so little, they found comfort in being able to afford fine objects.

The doors to the drawing room opened and Harry came in, still exuding an air of barely-suppressed excitement.

'Ready to eat, Ma?' he said, extending a hand.

'I'd like to know what's put you in such a good mood first,' she said, rising from her chair.

Harry gave a broad smile. 'I've had a good day. A great day. Something really wonderful happened.'

Lois wondered if at last Harry had persuaded Marshall Field to make him a partner. It was something he had wanted for so long and made sense since Harry was almost single-handedly responsible for ensuring the store stayed ahead of its competitors. Without Harry, Marshall Field would still be a fine store but a rather less go-ahead one. Lois knew how much Field appreciated Harry, yet at the same time he had proved reluctant to make him anything more than a valued and well-paid employee. In the long run, that was never going to be enough for her ambitious son who constantly drove the business forward. Lois smiled to herself. No wonder they called him Mile-A-Minute-Harry. She said, 'I'm guessing this "something wonderful" had to be more than a good day's takings.'

Harry could not wipe the smile from his face. 'Mother, tonight I'm not even going to mention the takings.'

'Now you have me really intrigued.'

Over dinner, Harry told his mother about finding Rosalie Buckingham alone in the restaurant, and how he had felt drawn to her.

'She really is a smart woman – warm too. And funny.' He remembered the almost teasing tone she had used when she spoke of stealing his idea and planting American Beauty roses at the Hyde Park development. A vision of her flashed through his mind – the amber eyes, the luminous skin, the wide, open smile – and, without realizing it, his expression softened. No doubt about it, Rose had made a powerful impression. He could not have put his finger on precisely why but he knew it, simply from how he felt inside.

'The way you're talking, this Rosalie Buckingham must be one special woman,' Lois said.

Harry nodded, his expression solemn all of a sudden. 'Rose – she asked me to call her Rose.'

Lois had never seen her son act this way over a woman. It was as if he had fallen under some kind of spell when it came to Rosalie Buckingham. *Rose.* Harry was never short of female company but, as far as Lois had been able to tell, there had not so far been anyone significant in his life. No one he would have considered settling down with or bringing home for his mother to meet, at any rate. Lois had never even known him talk to her in such a fashion about a woman. Usually, his conversation was to do with who had been shopping in the store or who was hosting such and such a party; nothing more than that. When it came to society events, he had no regular partner and often chose to take his mother. Lois did sometimes wonder if her presence in her son's life was making it difficult for him to consider marriage, simply because his loyalty to her was so great that he would never consider abandoning her. It had been a source of some sadness since what she most wanted was to see him married and with a family of his own. She regarded him with some curiosity now as he ate. Clearly, Rosalie – *Rose* – had made quite an impression.

'So tell me what else you know about Rose,' she said.

He did not need much prompting and every scrap of information he could bring to mind came pouring out. Rose was from one of Chicago's best families and following the death of her father, Benjamin, had inherited a large sum of money. She was a former debutante but not inclined to idle away her time.

'She's incredibly hard-working,' Harry said. 'This property development has occupied almost every waking moment for the best part of a year and now she has bought another prime piece of land to build on.' He was full of admiration. 'She has all kinds of plans, the kind of ideas that will really expand her business.'

Lois was amused. 'Who does that remind me of?' she said.

'It was lucky I even saw her today. It's the first day she hasn't been working for the longest time. She was practically forced to take a break by her business partner, her sister's husband, before she got burnt out.'

'I can think of another person who could use a day off here and there.'

Harry gave a shrug. 'Oh, I'm fine. I love what I do, you know that.'

'All the same, there's more to life than work.'

'You're right. That's why I asked Rose to come with me to the gala opening of the Monet exhibition next week.'

'I take it from the size of that smile of yours she accepted your invitation?'

He felt an urge to blurt out to Lois just how he felt about Rose, although in fact there was no need since she had already worked it out. His mind galloped ahead in its customary fashion, imagining a future that most certainly included Rose Buckingham. At the same time, it seemed crazy to him that a woman he had only just met and spent barely an hour in the company of could have had such a powerful effect that in his imagination he was already thinking way beyond the looming Monet exhibition.

In the end, he kept to himself much of what was going on inside his head. 'I'm keen on her,' he said. 'There's something about her, something …' he gave a helpless shrug and shot an awkward look at Lois. 'I can't even explain but I can *feel* it, if that makes any sense.' He placed a hand on his heart. 'Here, inside. I know it sounds crazy, as if I've gone and fallen head over feet for someone I've only just met.' He frowned. 'Am I making any sense?'

Lois knew exactly what he meant. She didn't think it crazy at all. It was how she had felt when she met Harry's father. All she had to do was think about him and something fluttered inside. She had thought they would be together always. Even now, almost thirty years after he had gone off to fight, she still expected him to show up on the doorstep. She could not accept that he was dead. Missing in action – that was the official explanation for him not coming back from the war. Missing, not dead. She took the distinction to mean there was still hope. It was what she chose to believe. Holding onto hope in the face of poor odds was the stuff of love. She had chosen to tell her son his father died in action, a hero. It had seemed to her kinder to give him the certainty she herself did not have. She gazed at Harry and saw the hope now shining in his eyes and wished she could somehow bestow on him all the happiness he wanted with none of the pain that being in love could bring. Sadly, he would have to find out for himself.

'If that's how you feel, then you must follow your heart and be happy,' she said.

He reached across the table and gave her hand a squeeze. Just then, unexpectedly, he felt a familiar sadness that was never far away cast its long shadow over his happiness, and wished his father was there to see what he had become and the direction in which his heart was now taking him.

3.

Rose Buckingham sat at the dressing table and began unpinning her hair. Perched on the end of her bed was her sister, Anna.

'Tell me again,' Anna said. 'Everything.'

Rose smiled at the expression on her big sister's concerned face reflected in the mirror. 'How many times, Anna? He asked me to go to the opening of the Monet exhibition, that's all.'

She untwisted a glossy coil of dark hair and deposited several hair grips in a glass bowl on the dressing table. As she pulled a brush through her hair she thought about her encounter with Harry Selfridge, his unexpected invitation to the gala night, and wondered if he was merely being polite since she had expressed an interest in art. No, it was more than that. She had seen the way he looked at her. To her surprise, she had felt her insides knotting up as they talked. She knew what it meant, that there was a spark there, what her sister called chemistry. She smiled at the recollection. Anna got up from the bed and leaned against the edge of the dressing table, arms folded, facing her.

'There's something you're not telling me. I can see it in your eyes.'

Rose stopped brushing her hair and gazed up at Anna. 'It's only a feeling,' she said.

'What kind of a feeling?'

Rose laughed, thinking back to the way Harry had studied her, the intensity in his dark eyes. She still wasn't sure what colour they were; brown, most likely, although such a deep shade of mahogany as to be almost black. They were eyes that had felt pain, she could see that, but the lines that appeared at the corners when he smiled told her that he was also a man who knew how to enjoy life. He had exuded a great warmth and in his company she had felt her heart rate become more rapid. She wanted to say this to Anna, explain how he had made her feel inside.

'I liked him,' she said, eventually, keeping her tone mild.

Anna frowned. 'I knew it.'

Rose shook her head. 'No point getting carried away, anyway. I've only just met him.'

'It's not as if he's a stranger, though, is it? I mean everybody knows Harry Selfridge.'

'I suppose they do – is that a good thing?'

'It means what you see is what you get. There's no façade. He started low down and worked his way up. By all accounts, Marshall Field thinks highly of him, which says something. If he's willing to put his faith in a man like Selfridge ...' she left the rest of the sentence hanging in the air.

Rose bristled. 'Hold on – "a man like Selfridge" – what exactly does that mean?'

'Don't take this the wrong way but it's not as if he's from a good family. You do know that some people call him Marshall Field's office boy.' Anna hesitated. 'I heard he was turned down by the Chicago Club. Not considered the right sort.'

Rose was indignant. Her father had been a member of the exclusive Chicago Club. It was a traditional place, cliquey, as far as she could tell. Benjamin Buckingham, while aware of its shortcomings, had found it useful in terms of business connections. Her heart went out to Harry. She could well imagine Chicago's old money set viewing him as something of an upstart. 'If you're right, they missed out. Harry could have given that stuffy bunch a thing or two to think about.'

'That's probably what worried them.'

'Pity Father's not here. He could have put a word in.'

Anna wasn't so sure about that. 'I'm not trying to put you off, sis, just saying it might be an idea to take a step back and think about who you're really getting involved with here. Harry Selfridge doesn't have a pedigree-'

A shocked Rose cut her short. '*Pedigree*? Anna, have you any idea how snobbish that sounds?'

'I don't mean to be. I just think you deserve the best, that's all.'

'He's taking me to an art exhibition, not marrying me. It might be the last I ever see of him.' She doubted it but her sister's reservations regarding Harry Selfridge's suitability made her wary about giving away the true extent of her feelings.

Where Harry was concerned, Rose shared none of her sister's qualms. So far. She preferred to make up her mind based on her own experiences rather than whatever the prevailing tittle-tattle happened to be. That was not to say she was unaware of what Chicago thought about Harry. He was too big a character not to provoke gossip. On the one hand, he was much admired for his business acumen, for carving out a successful career purely on the basis of effort and talent. There was no one else in town like him, no doubt about it. On the other hand, he was said to indulge in high stakes poker at the infamous houses where so-called ladies of the night plied their trade. She was not about to judge him. How he behaved towards her – that was what counted. It alone would tell her what kind of man he really was. As far as she was concerned, the fact she came from one of the 'best' families in Chicago – whatever that meant – was neither here nor there. That she had been born into money and privilege and all her life mixed with what many considered the cream of society was of no consequence. Money and status were often a poor indicator of kindness and integrity, she had found. Some of the least interesting people she had met were also the most successful. She knew, however, that the roots of the class system went deep and that many who moved in the same circles as she did would consider Harry Selfridge to be inferior.

Already, she sensed that her mother shared Anna's concerns. Martha Buckingham had looked baffled when Rose explained about running into Harry at the store, their conversation about art, his invitation to go with him to the Monet opening.

'Is it altogether wise when you don't know the man?'

When Rose retorted she would never get to know him unless she spent time with him her mother had been unable to disguise her anxiety. Thinking about it, she had also said something about Rose deserving the very best, somehow implying that Harry was not quite up to scratch.

Anna broke into her thoughts. 'Don't forget you're coming for dinner the weekend after next. Hyde Park is almost at the halfway stage, thanks to you and Frank almost working yourselves into the ground. It's time we took a moment to celebrate.'

'It's a lovely idea. I hadn't forgotten.'

'Oh, did I say, I've asked Tyler to come along too?' Anna tried to keep her voice casual.

Rose was put out. 'No, you did not say. Please tell me you're not trying to set the two of us up.'

'I just think you could give him a chance.'

Rose sighed, exasperated. Tyler Collins was a gifted architect and they had an excellent working relationship. He was reliable and good-humoured, willing to put in as many hours as Rose and Frank to make the project a success. On more than one occasion Rose had wondered how far Hyde Park would have got had it not been for his input and calming influence. Although she was fond of him, lately she had begun to suspect his feelings for her were straying beyond those of colleagues. Once or twice it had seemed that Frank, her brother-in-law, had made excuses to leave Rose and Tyler alone in the office. Now she had the distinct impression her sister's celebratory dinner was a ruse to throw the two of them together. If so, Anna would be disappointed.

'It's not fair to make him think I'm interested when I'm not,' Rose said.

'You can't be sure. Until you spend some time with him – real time, away from plans and costings and discussions about brickwork and floors and heaven knows what – you'll never know.'

She did, though, that was the point. It didn't actually take long to work out whether or not the air crackled with excitement when you were with someone. It either did or it didn't. She had known in an instant with Harry and yet had worked closely with Tyler for months and felt nothing more than friendship for him. Dinner was not going to change that.

'Keep an open mind, that's all I ask,' Anna said.

Rose said she would even though she knew deep down that her sister's efforts at matchmaking were a waste of time.

4.

Harry arrived at Marshall Field an hour earlier than usual with a definite spring in his step. It was a glorious morning, sun beating down from a cloudless sky, and he got his driver to drop him a couple of blocks away – in part so that he could take the air, but also because he felt the need to *do* something rather than sit in the carriage while his mind whirred and adrenaline pumped through his system, making him eager to get on with the day. The way he was feeling was all to do with Rose Buckingham, he was sure of it. At the forefront of his mind was the Monet exhibition. He had written to her, a formal invitation, and had one of the lads in the accounts department take it to her home. It had required all his willpower not to send an ostentatious bouquet of roses too. The last thing he wanted to do was appear so eager as to come across as off-putting.

Harry strolled past the front of the store, taking in the window displays that marked the forthcoming Monet exhibition. The theme had been colour and light and the head of the art department, Cecil Crisp, had done an outstanding job. Swathes of fabric in yellows and oranges, reds and pinks, adorned each window. There was a dramatic scene in blue and turquoise, inky shades of purple evocative of a starlit night. The shop front was looking the best Harry had ever seen it. Cecil Crisp's interpretation of Impressionist art had brought home to Harry the beauty of it in a way he had not managed to appreciate hitherto. He was beginning to understand what Rose saw in the paintings. His spirit soared even higher at the thought of seeing her again.

At the end of the block he turned the corner and went round the back of the building where the loading bay was open and staff in fawn jackets and caps unpacked deliveries for despatch to the various departments. He looked around and it struck him that amongst the men and youngsters sorting the stock there could well be someone with the same ambitions he had starting out. His own experience had taught him that, no matter how humble your background, anything was possible. His success proved you didn't need the advantages the upper echelons of society afforded its own in order to make it. The fact that some of the old traditionalists looked down their noses at him was something he chose to sweep aside. Harry knew his worth and remained as ambitious as ever, determined that one day he would have a store of his own.

In the far corner of the vast loading bay some of the younger lads were in a huddle making a racket, exchanging good-humoured banter. When one of them looked over his shoulder and spotted Harry watching he hissed a warning to the rest and the chat died down at once. Harry put up his hands as if to say it was OK, he wasn't checking up on them.

So long as the work got done and things didn't get out of hand, he was not inclined to give the workers a hard time for having fun. It was his firm belief that a happy workforce was a productive one.

'Gentlemen, don't let me interrupt,' he said, heading towards the little group.

At the centre of the gathering was one of the junior packers, Danny Donovan, who had joined the store a couple of years previously and proved reliable and hard-working. He was flushed with excitement.

'Looks like I just walked in on a celebration,' Harry said, seeing the looks on the faces of the others.

Danny Donovan glanced about him. His lanky frame seemed dwarfed by the buff jacket the loading bay staff were required to wear. He fiddled with the knot of his tie, awkward, not managing to keep the smile from his face. 'I'm getting married, Mr Selfridge,' he blurted out, his cheeks growing even more pink.

Harry grinned. 'That most certainly is cause to celebrate, Danny. And do we know the lucky lady – does she also work here at the store?'

'No, sir. At the bakery near where we live, over on Clark Street. I've known her all my life.'

The lad next to him aimed a playful dig at his ribs. 'Never going to go hungry with your Clara's baking, are you, Danny?'

The others laughed.

By Harry's reckoning, Danny Donovan was twenty years old, yet had a softness about him, an innocence, almost, that made him appear much younger. It got Harry thinking about what he had been like at that age. Not harder-edged, exactly, but more resilient, perhaps. Certainly, more mature-looking. He had grown up fast; had to. For as long as he could remember so much had been riding on him making a go of things he had felt the need to push and push himself. Failure had never been an option. At the age of twenty, Harry was already on a mission to provide for his mother and at the same time make his name. It went through his mind that had the father he so desperately missed returned from war after all his own hunger for success might well have been diminished. He might not have felt the same desperate need to do so well.

'I wish you every happiness, Danny,' he said. 'Set a date for the big day, yet?'

'We're looking at November, Mr Selfridge, all being well.'

'Good luck to you – and to Clara.'

Harry moved off along the narrow corridor that led to the deserted shop floor and wandered among the displays, running a finger over counters and ledges, checking that everything was as it should be. It was his habit to leave his initials, HGS – Harry Gordon Selfridge – on any dusty surface he found, but everything appeared gleaming and in good order. For a moment, he stood in the centre of the store, surveying his surroundings, enjoying a rare moment of silence. It was his input that had helped make the store a leader in its field. Whilst Marshall Field was an astute businessman he had already accumulated his fortune and did not therefore have anywhere near the same drive as Harry. Field was less interested than his right-hand man in travelling the world, seeing how other leading stores were modernizing themselves, and going one better than the competition. Nor did he have Harry's flair for putting on a show. Among Chicago's business community Harry was regarded as a match for the great showman, Barnum. When one of the newspapers picked up on the story and ran a piece asking if shopping was now entering the realms of theatre at Marshall Field, Harry could not have been more pleased. It was exactly the impact he wanted to create. He felt his efforts deserved more than the senior position he occupied with its generous salary. He wanted to be a partner – something he felt he had more than earned. He intended to raise the subject at his meeting with Marshall Field later that day. Nothing would make him happier than to win round his employer on the eve of taking Rose to the Monet opening,

He strolled among the gleaming cabinets and display units. In less than a couple of hours, once the doors opened for business, the place would come to life. For now, the store was sleeping, readying itself for all the day would bring. Taking one last look, he sprinted up the staircase that led to the upper floor and offices, eager for the day to begin.

5.

Rose was at her desk early. In front of her was a set of plans. She was meant to be thinking about the community aspect of the Harper Lane development, the area where the neighbourhood grocery and drugstore would go, along with a café and space for books and reading. There was even going to be a hall where residents could gather and stage their own events. She felt some impatience to get everything completed before the last houses went up, wanting the people who moved in to have a sense right from the outset that this was no ordinary place to live. She imagined a vibrant enclave filled with creative people who had in common a real sense of community spirit.

The night before, she had not slept well, thinking about the layout of the community block, wondering if it was right to have the drugstore in the middle and the café at one end. She could not help thinking the café should be at the heart of things. People would always go that little bit further to the drugstore but might not bother to visit a café, she reasoned. Now, waiting for Frank to arrive in the office and eager to discuss it with him, she felt less sure. She couldn't help wondering what Harry Selfridge would do. Perhaps, if she was still uncertain, she could get his opinion when she saw him the following evening. She sat back in her chair and ran a hand over her hair. A strand had come loose and she pinned it back in place. Harry. She imagined him at Marshall Field, patrolling the store, checking on the restaurant, making sure the place ran like clockwork and that every customer who came through the doors had the best shopping experience possible. What had he said? The customer is always right. She liked that. It was a sign of humility, of wanting to ensure great service. It meant the Marshall Field ethos was built on respect, which was something she also applied to her own business. Every property that bore her name had to be of a standard, somewhere she herself would be proud to call home. Building houses that had no heart held no interest for her. Whenever she thought about the people moving into Harper Lane she felt protective and wanted them to be happy. Like Harry, she wanted them to feel everything had been done to make their purchase right for them.

She wanted the spirit of the development to be upbeat.

She heard the outer door open and looked up, expecting to see her brother-in-law walk in. Instead of Frank, Tyler Collins appeared. Rose felt her heart sink and at once felt guilty for reacting so negatively. Tyler was a decent man and a first-rate architect. It was hardly his fault her sister was trying to pair them up. She managed a warm smile.

'You're early,' she said, working hard at sounding pleased to see him. 'Did you have trouble sleeping too?'

Tyler gave her a look of concern. 'You're not sleeping? How come? Not worried about the development, I hope, because you really don't have to be. Everything is on track and looking good.'

She wished she hadn't said anything. The last thing she wanted was Tyler taking anything other than a professional interest in her. 'Oh, I woke a little early, that's all, and it's such a beautiful morning I thought I might as well head on out and make a start.'

He came over to her desk and glanced at the plans in front of her. 'Is there a problem with the community buildings?'

'No, nothing at all. I just had some thoughts going round inside my head and decided to take another look, make sure everything was exactly the way it should be.' She decided not to mention anything about switching round the drugstore and the café at this stage. No sense stirring things up until she was absolutely sure. 'You know how it is when something takes hold, especially in the early hours. All it is, we've been so busy lately I don't feel I've had time to take a step back and *think*. I guess when work is all you're doing you don't always get things clear. It's good to have a moment to reflect sometimes, wouldn't you say?'

Tyler brightened. 'I couldn't agree more. We've all been working hard, putting in the hours, you more than anyone. You could use a breather. We all could. I was about to ask if you'd come with me to the opening of the Monet exhibition tomorrow. Short notice, I know, but I've only just managed to get my name on the guest list. It's popular. Looks like the whole of Chicago will be there. How about it?'

She tried hard to hide her dismay. Not for a second had she dreamed Tyler would ask to take her out. Struggling to keep her composure, she said, 'That's so kind of you, Tyler, but really I can't-'

He jumped in. 'Come on. Rosalie, you'll love it. I know how much you love painting. You can't believe how many strings I had to pull to get on that guest list.'

He looked so pleased with himself she felt awful. There was no easy way to tell him. 'I know, and I'm grateful. It's just ...' she wasn't sure how to say she was already going. With Harry Selfridge. 'I already have plans to go,' she said, hoping Tyler would leave it at that.

'I'm sorry, I had no idea. I should have known your mother would get an invite, since she's such a patron of the arts.'

It stung her to think he would automatically assume her companion was her *mother*. Was that how she appeared – some kind of old maid? 'Actually, Mother wasn't invited. I'm going as the guest of Harry Selfridge.' There, she had said it.

Tyler seemed utterly perplexed, so much so that Rose wasn't sure he knew who Harry was. She was about to explain when he said, 'You mean, the Marshall Field man?'

Something in the way he said it let Rose know he was less than impressed.

'That's right, Marshall Field's right-hand man.' She put the emphasis on *right-hand*, just so there could be no misunderstanding her own feelings.

Tyler said nothing. He seemed knocked off balance for a moment and went and sat at his own desk. He took off his glasses and rubbed them with a crumpled handkerchief. When he looked up again Rose saw the disappointment in his pale blue eyes and felt a stab of sympathy.

'I'm really sorry. It's kind of you to ask. You must go – take someone else.'

He replaced the glasses, pushing them up onto the bridge of his nose. 'If there's anything in those plans you wanted to run past me, now would be a good time,' he said, no longer so friendly.

I've hurt his feelings, she thought. 'Maybe later,' she said, and went back to poring over the plans.

6.

Not for the first time, Harry wondered how Marshall Field could be content with such a poky office. There wasn't room for much more than the desk which, admittedly, was a large and impressive-looking affair, a narrow glass-fronted bookcase, and a single hard-backed chair reserved for visitors. Harry went out of his way to spend as little time as possible with his boss and remained on his feet if he could since the visitor's chair was a rickety thing, given to pitching about. One of these days, Harry was convinced it would collapse underneath some unfortunate person. As long as it wasn't him.

At least Field allowed himself a more comfortable seat, more armchair than utilitarian office furniture. Harry went over to the window while he waited for his boss to appear. The view wasn't even of State Street but instead the grubby warehouse across the alley at the back of the store. Harry shook his head. It was hard to know what really made Marshall Field tick. Generating profit had to be a major part of it, presumably, since he was one of Chicago's wealthiest individuals, from old money. If you didn't know it, however, you would be hard-pressed to work out just how well off he was. From what Harry could tell, Field eschewed the more obvious trappings of wealth. There was his office for a start, the least expansive in the whole store. Then there was his home, which was large but by no means one of the biggest in the city. As for his clothes ... Marshall Field wore understated suits, always the same flat brown in colour; designed, it seemed, to go unnoticed. In almost every respect, he and Harry had nothing in common. If Harry had Marshall Field's money he would be letting the world know about it. After all, what was the point of working so hard to generate great wealth if you didn't know how to spend it?

The door creaked open and Marshall Field came in. He really was drab-looking, from his hair to his complexion and clothing.

'I'm not late, am I?' he said, straightening the blotter on his desk and gesturing for Harry to sit down.

He was never late. Harry shook his head. 'Not at all.'

'I just swung by the restaurant, wanted to see how it was doing once the lunch trade was over. What you said about it always being full – you're right. Every table occupied and, according to the manager, that's how it is all day, every day.'

'We need to expand,' Harry said. He was working up some figures and would soon be ready to present his case.

'I agree. Good work, Selfridge. I'll leave it to you to decide how we do it.'

Harry gave a broad smile. The degree of confidence his boss had in him was always encouraging. Well-timed too, since he was about to broach a rather delicate subject.

'If that's all, I'm going to call it a day,' Marshall Field said, catching Harry off guard.

'A few more minutes of your time, if I may,' he said.

Marshall Field settled back into the chair and rested his elbows on the padded leather arms. He seemed tired, his skin more pallid than usual. Increasingly, he was leaving the office mid-afternoon, perhaps because a full day behind his desk was simply too much.

'The store's doing really well,' Harry began. 'The latest figures show we're up across all departments. The restaurant's a success, the bargain lines in the basement are proving popular. I think we've got things right. Marshall Field is Chicago's premier store.' He paused for effect. 'And this is just the beginning. There's so much more we can do. I've plenty of ideas.'

Marshall Field gave a nod, in no doubt it was Harry Selfridge's enthusiasm and flair for retail that lay at the heart of the store's burgeoning success.

'I'm happy here,' Harry went on. 'I love my job and the reason I'm able to do it so well is because you give me all the freedom I need. I know that and I want you to know I appreciate it very much. Your allowing me free-rein is instrumental to the improvements and the increased revenue we've seen this past year.'

Again, Marshall Field nodded.

Harry was getting into his stride. 'I can't think of anywhere I'd rather be than right here-'

'I sense a "but" coming up.'

'But *I* want to develop too, just like the store. I see myself as more than an employee.' He took a deep breath. 'The way I feel about the store, I care about it. It's more than a job to me. It's my passion, if you can understand that.' Another breath. 'I want a stake in it. I want to be a partner. Each day when I step into the building I want to know a part of it is *mine*. When I walk the floor I want every single person who works here or shops here to know it too.'

Marshall Field's expression gave nothing away.

Harry sat forward in his chair. 'You know my value. I do too.' Despite the fact it was common knowledge that Marshall Field held him in high esteem, Harry knew there were still those in Chicago society who saw him as an imposter. He had heard the 'office boy' jibes and no matter how hard he tried to ignore them they stung. If Field made him a partner, it would silence the critics once and for all.

'I do my job well – too well to be content to draw a salary every month. I need more – and, in all honesty, I think I *deserve* more. What do you say?'

7.

Rose was on edge. She paced back and forth in the lobby as she waited for Harry to arrive to take her to the Monet exhibition. Every so often, her hand flew up to check that her hair was in place and not escaping the pins designed to keep her curls in order. She wished Anna was here to give her a pep talk and calm her nerves. Then again, Anna was not perhaps the best person. Hadn't she tried to talk Rose out of going to the event with Harry in the first place? Granted, she had been less critical since voicing her initial reservations but all the same. Rose suspected that her sister secretly hoped the evening would not be a success. She turned to see her mother descend the sweeping oak staircase. Rose gave her a tense smile.

'You're going to wear out the pattern on those tiles if you keep on with all that walking up and down,' Martha Buckingham said.

'Do I look all right?'

Her mother stood in front of her and looked her daughter up and down, scrutinizing every inch. Rose frowned. 'Is something wrong?' Again, the hand checking the back of her hair.

'You look quite radiant,' Martha said. 'That colour is perfect on you.'

Rose had chosen the dark red shot silk gown because it was almost the same shade as the rose on the table of the restaurant at Marshall Field, not that she would have admitted to such sentimentality. 'I haven't worn it for a while,' she said. 'I hope it's suitable.'

At her throat, Rose wore a heavy necklace, an intricate design of rubies and diamonds. She had on earrings that went with it. Both pieces had come from London originally and had been made for her great-grandmother. Rose and her sister had been fortunate to inherit some wonderful pieces of jewellery that had been in the family for generations.

'The rubies look good on you,' her mother said, reaching up and touching her daughter's cheek.

'Are they too much?' She had worried that so many precious stones were ostentatious, that Harry might think she was parading her family wealth. She didn't want him to be intimidated. Then again, it was hard to imagine a man with the confidence and self-belief of Harry Selfridge being thrown by a few precious stones.

'I get the feeling you have a soft spot for this Selfridge chap,' Martha said, giving her daughter a searching look. 'Seems he must have something special about him.'

'He's an interesting man,' Rose said, doing her best to sound less interested than she really was.

The doorbell chimed. Rose shot her mother a look of panic.

'Relax,' Martha said, amused, as their butler, Forman, went to open the door. Harry was ushered into an entrance hall that could have doubled as a ballroom it was so vast. In an instant he registered the paintings and wall hangings on the staircase, the chaise-longue and side tables inlaid with what might have been ivory. His first view of the house from the outside had made quite an impact. The fancy little turrets and stained glass leaded windows caught his eye at once. So well-screened from the road was the property, hidden behind tall Sycamore trees, that it was only as the carriage pulled onto the drive that Harry was able to appreciate the scale of the place. It had to be one of the grander family homes in all of Chicago. His own house, lovely though it was, was not in the same league. Nowhere near. For a moment it crossed his mind that he was being foolish thinking a woman like Rose would be interested in him. Then something his mother had said for as long as he could remember came back to him: 'You're as good as the next man,' Lois insisted. 'Don't ever let anyone tell you you're not.'

'I *am* good enough,' he said under his breath, as the carriage drew to a halt at the front of the mansion.

The sight of Rose in an exquisite dress in crimson silk trimmed with lace took his breath away. At her throat, diamonds and blood-red rubies glinted in the light. For a moment he was almost lost for words, then recovered and strode forward, presenting her with a bouquet of fragrant roses. 'You look really wonderful, Rose,' he said.

'Harry, this is my mother.'

'Mrs Buckingham, I'm very pleased to meet you.'

She gave a nod. She had heard the stories about Harry Selfridge, the barbed 'office boy' comments and, although she had not said as much, based on what she knew, she had not deemed him suitable company for her daughter. Now, however, seeing the look on Rose's face, the unashamed delight in his eyes at the sight of her, she realized the wise course of action would be to keep a more open mind.

'Rosalie has been so looking forward to the exhibition.' She glanced in her daughter's direction. 'Monet must be quite something to have caused such excitement. She has talked of little else this past week.' Rose looked away, hoping her mother wasn't about to embarrass her. 'She is something of a painter herself, you know.'

'She told me. I look forward to seeing some of her work one of these days.'

'She's actually very talented – a good deal better than she will ever tell you.'

'Mother, please …' Rose shot a pleading look at Harry. 'Shouldn't we be leaving?'

'Of course. I can see you're keen to get a look at those paintings, Rose. Goodnight, Mrs Buckingham.'

Rose. Martha Buckingham watched her daughter take Harry Selfridge's arm. 'I do hope you will look after her well, Mr Selfridge.' She gave him a cool, appraising look. 'She's very precious to me.'

The warning implicit in her words was clear, leaving Harry in no doubt he would have his work cut out to win over the Buckingham family.

8.

Harry and Rose stood in front of a striking painting awash with yellow and pink. It seemed to cast brilliant rays of sunshine into the room. Harry stole a look at Rose and saw in her expression the same sense of delight he had detected the day he approached her in the restaurant at the store. She was utterly entranced. He remained quiet, waiting for her to break the silence.

'Such a gift to be able to create such wonders on the canvas,' she said, eventually.

Harry agreed. He might not have been able to explain why he liked the paintings but he could appreciate their beauty.

'Are you having a good time?' he said.

She laughed. 'Wonderful. Thank you for inviting me.'

The opening had drawn hundreds of guests, many of whom Harry knew, or at least recognized. Most shopped at Marshall Field. Some belonged to what he thought of as the creative crowd; actors and writers, artists of one sort or another. A skinny figure with unruly hair and a moustache that could have done with a trim came over. His russet corduroy suit was in sharp contrast to the smart evening attire of the other men in the gallery. When Harry saw him, he gave a warm smile. His old friend, Lawrence Porter, now making a name for himself as a landscape painter. Harry had commissioned him to do a series of murals throughout the store the previous year for Thanksgiving and in the process had helped raise his profile considerably. Porter had since staged well-received exhibitions in Chicago and New York.

'Harry! I didn't expect to see you,' he said. 'Surely you're not here for the art.' He gave Rose a conspiratorial wink. 'The man's a workaholic, never stops. It's nigh on impossible to drag him away from that blessed store – certainly not to look at paintings. I really can't imagine how you managed it.'

Harry grinned. 'You're making me out to be awfully dull, Lawrence.' He turned to Rose. 'This is my good friend, Lawrence Porter. Lawrence, meet Miss Rose Buckingham.'

Lawrence gave a formal bow. 'It's an honour.'

'*The* Lawrence Porter?' Rose said. 'I saw your work at the Charlton Gallery. You have a real gift.'

Lawrence gave a modest shrug. 'That's kind of you. I'm certainly doing a lot better these days than I was a year ago when interest in me was pitiful. Some of Harry's business sense must have rubbed off because since the two of us met I've never looked back.' He gave a mischievous grin. 'No more starving artist in a freezing garret. I can actually afford to eat these days.'

'Very pleased to hear it.' Harry looked him up and down, noting the slim frame. 'It looks to me as if you've not yet got the hang of feeding yourself properly so how about you let me buy you dinner one night.'

'See how easily I manage to prey on his generosity?' Lawrence told Rose. 'I only have to *appear* malnourished to wangle myself a decent meal in one of Chicago's finest restaurants.'

'We'll fix something up,' Harry said.

'Why not bring Miss Buckingham?'

Harry glanced at Rose. She seemed happy to be included. 'Rose, you would be most welcome – then at least one of us will know what he's talking about when he starts going on about his work. Which he will, believe me.'

'It will be a useful diversion when you start bringing up the ins and outs of the retail world,' Lawrence countered.

Rose intervened. 'Enough! Is this what an evening in the company of the two of you will be like? Endless sparring?'

Lawrence glanced at Harry. 'Afraid so,' he said.

Harry laughed. 'It's only fair to warn you there may be some refereeing to be done, if that's OK with you.'

Rose was amused. 'As long as we can all agree the referee has the last word.'

'Agreed,' Harry and Lawrence said in unison.

From the other side of the room this exchange was being observed. After being turned down by Rose, Tyler Collins had come to the opening on his own and wandered among the other guests, all of whom seemed to be accompanied. He had taken full advantage of the champagne that was on offer and, not having eaten, was feeling the worse for wear. Seeing Rose having such a good time only served to further darken his mood. He replaced his empty glass on a tray and helped himself to another drink, draining half of it at once. He had never seen Rose so animated. She was clearly enchanted with the company of Selfridge and the scruffy individual who had joined them. Fancy coming to a formal event in a tatty old suit that would be more at home at a fairground. If that was the sort Selfridge mixed with then Rose really ought to watch her step. Tyler Collins waited until the scruff moved off and then headed over, slightly more unsteady on his feet than he had realized. He bumped against an elderly woman in a billowing blue gown and stiff hairdo and attracted disapproving looks from her silver-haired escort.

Rose had her back to him. She stood next to Harry Selfridge, so close that their shoulders touched. Tyler watched as she aimed a bright smile at her companion.

'Rosalie,' he said, his voice thick.

She spun around, surprised to see him. She did not seem altogether pleased, he noticed as he stood, champagne in hand, swaying ever so slightly, a soppy smile on his face.

Rose and Harry exchanged a look. She introduced the two men and explained that Tyler was the architect working on Harper Lane.

'I was hoping she would accompany me tonight but she already had plans,' Tyler said. Rose appeared dismayed as he pressed on. 'When she said she was going with Marshall Field's-' he paused, searching for the right word – 'sorry, it's on the tip of my tongue.' He frowned. 'Marshall Field's … *man*, that's right. I have to say I was surprised.'

Harry remained silent.

'Do you think we could get some air?' Rose asked Harry.

He gave a nod, took her arm. 'Excuse us,' he said and steered her away, out of the main gallery and through to the courtyard at the back of the building.

Tyler Collins, momentarily thrown, watched them go as they exited the room. 'Office boy,' he called out. 'That's the expression I was searching for.'

Several people turned and stared at the intoxicated man, unaccompanied, apparently talking to himself.

9.

'Harry, I am so sorry,' Rose said.

'It's not for you to apologize. He was drunk. A little too much champagne. I should have headed him off.' Harry had heard Collins hurl his insult as they headed out and was certain Rose had too. 'I'm only sorry you had to witness such bad manners. I guess he was upset you turned him down?'

He wanted to ask who Tyler Collins was to Rose; did she have feelings for him? Was there some kind of romantic history between the two of them that explained his behaviour? Harry was, he realized, jealous, as well as insulted. At the same time he was angry with himself, feeling he should somehow have been able to stop Tyler Collins from getting anywhere near. Not that he could have done – he'd have needed eyes in the back of his head. Still, he felt he had let Rose down. What had her mother said? That she expected him to take good care of her daughter. *She is very precious.* Once word got back that he had allowed an inebriated individual to get close enough to prove a nuisance Mrs Buckingham would probably never let him near her daughter again. Then again, perhaps Rose

MARIA MALONE

wouldn't want to see him anyway. It had all been going so well and now the mood of the night was ruined. He gazed up at the heavens at a blue-black sky crowded with stars. Feeling a hand on his arm he turned and saw Rose smiling.

'It's like standing beneath one of those paintings we've just been looking at,' she said. 'Don't you think?'

He turned his eyes heavenwards again and understood what she meant. He glanced at her.

'If we're lucky we might see a shooting star. Shall we sit for a moment?'

They found a bench under a tree strewn with tiny lanterns.

'You're not cold?' Harry said.

She shook her head. 'It's nice to be out in the air.'

Harry's mind was whirring. There was so much he wanted to say and yet, unaccountably, something held him back. Straight-talking Harry Selfridge, one of the most direct and fearless businessmen in all of Chicago, cowed in the presence of this gentle, lovely woman. She sat, straight-backed, her hands resting in her lap, half in shadow. A slight smile played on her lips. Harry could not shake the feeling he'd had the first time he had encountered her, the sense that his pulse was racing. Already he knew he wanted to keep seeing Rose, to never stop. With that in mind, he had to put things on a proper footing. He knew from business the value of having a good, strong foundation. A store with nothing solid at its base would never last. At the first sign of stress it would begin to crumble. If Harry was serious about Rose he would need to deal with the inevitable prejudices their relationship would meet with in Chicago. They had just had a taste of it with the outburst from Tyler Collins. *Office boy.* There would be others who felt the same, Harry had no doubt. He was loath to subject Rose to such disapproval. She deserved better. Then again, no matter what anyone else might think, he knew he was capable of giving her the best and defying the snobbish class system that pervaded some elements of the city's so-called elite. He had been brought up to make up his mind about people based on their qualities, not the family they came from. Whether they were the most junior employees at the store or leading lights of the business world made no difference to him. Harry wasn't a snob. His instincts were usually spot-on. He was able to get along with anyone. So long as they were decent, that was what mattered to him. Lawrence Porter had been on the way to becoming a down and out when Harry met him. It was the man he liked, his talent he respected. The fact he had holes in his shoes and a frayed shirt collar was neither here nor there. One of Harry's mottoes was to treat others as you would wish to be treated. It had served him pretty well so far.

He turned to Rose.

'There will always be people who see me as not good enough,' he began. 'No matter what I achieve they'll be more interested in where I came from and what I *don't* have than anything I do with my life.' He gazed at her. 'The last thing I want to do, Rose, is put you in a position where you feel embarrassed to be seen with me. It wouldn't be fair.' He was silent for a moment. 'What I'm saying is, now you've had time to think, I'll understand if you want to decline that dinner invitation with Lawrence Porter – and any other invitations I might extend.'

Rose let his words sink in. She put a hand on his.

'Harry, I couldn't care what anyone else thinks. Sitting here under the stars just now got me thinking about my father. I was a little girl when he passed away and my mother has been alone ever since. Not a day goes by that she doesn't miss him. I can see it in her eyes, in everything she does, that he is still on her mind. What I'm trying to say is that life is short and we none of us know what's coming our way, good or bad, so all we can do is be happy and trust our feelings. How do we know if something's right? It feels good. How do we know when it's wrong? It feels bad.' She gave a shrug. 'Being here with you feels *good*.' She gave his hand a squeeze, let go. 'And don't think you can get out of taking me along to that dinner with Lawrence Porter – the two of you aren't safe to be left alone together.'

10.

For almost a week it had suited Rose to do whatever work was required at home. She found she could manage perfectly well not going into the office and enjoyed being able to stroll in the garden, thinking and sketching. The Monet exhibition had got her fired up and she was painting again, not the precise figurative work she had been doing before, something less restrained and full of bright splashes of colour. She was letting her imagination run riot, letting go of the thoughtful approach she had previously favoured and seeing where her work took her. She wasn't sure if what she was doing was any good but she didn't mind. The mere act of painting was giving her great pleasure, more so than she could ever recall. She had chosen as her subject the yellow climbing roses that covered the wall at the back of the garden next to the summerhouse. The brickwork they clung to was a weathered terracotta, the latticework of the summerhouse painted in a delicate shade of yellow. Rose was playing with colour and light and texture. The flowers spread across the canvas, only a hint of the summerhouse visible on the very edge of the picture. She would never have thought of painting this way had it not been for the exhibition. The evening had truly inspired her, and not just in terms of her art. She had made up her mind about Harry, judging him to be good company. She admired his spirit. The fact he had come from nothing made him *more* attractive as far as she was concerned. He had earned his success, not had it handed to him on a silver plate, like so many of her contemporaries. Rose put down her brush and took a few steps back from the easel. She had no pretensions to be any kind of an artist but all the same she liked the way the painting was coming along. She stretched, rubbed at a knot of tension at the back of her neck and caught sight of her mother crossing the lawn, coming her way.

'Don't look, Mother,' Rose said, making a half-hearted attempt to hide the painting. 'It's not finished.'

Martha Buckingham came over. 'If you really don't want me to see it I promise I won't peep, but you should know I did get a glimpse before you stepped in front of it.'

Rose laughed. 'I don't mind, not really. Just don't expect too much.'

She stepped aside and Martha took a step closer, examining her daughter's efforts. 'I'm not much of an expert,' she said at last, 'but I know what I like. It's unusual, but it's good. The colours are quite something.'

The women sat in the shade of the summerhouse facing the rose-strewn wall.

'It's good to see you taking some time away from the office,' Martha said. 'You've been working much too hard.'

'I'm not neglecting my responsibilities, just managing my time a little better,' Rose said. 'It's strange but for some reason it seems I'm able to accomplish so much more at the moment than I was before. Work, my painting – there's room for both. I think perhaps I had become a little too focused on work to the exclusion of all else.'

She wasn't about to admit to her mother that the real reason she was staying away from the office was that she was not yet ready to face Tyler Collins after what had happened at the gala opening. His behaviour had been embarrassing and completely out of character from what Rose knew of him. The day after his tipsy outburst when she had decided not to go into work he had sent a note of apology, begging forgiveness. She had chosen to be gracious and had written back to say, for the sake of their working relationship, she was willing to accept his apology and draw a line under the incident.

'You know, Rose, you seem very much happier these past few days,' Martha said. 'There's a real glow about you, a sparkle in your eyes. I'm very glad to see you like this.' Rose smiled. 'I can't help thinking it must be something to do with that art exhibition. It seems to have utterly transformed you. I must get along to see it myself, see if it can do the same for me.'

Rose knew what her mother was doing; fishing, wanting Rose to admit that the real reason she was radiating such joy was not in fact sparked by the delights of the exhibition at all but by the company of Harry Selfridge.

When Rose said nothing, Martha went on. 'Of course, I could be on the wrong track entirely. Perhaps the paintings, no doubt lovely, paled in comparison to the charms of your companion.'

Rose could not contain herself and burst out laughing. 'Mother, you are incorrigible. And since you ask, my happiness is in part down to Monet and in part to Harry Selfridge.'

'I've been making some enquiries-'

'-Please, Mother, don't interfere. I am almost thirty years old, for goodness sake.'

'And you will always be my little girl, just as your sister is, even though she has a husband and a home of her own. A mother's responsibilities don't end once their child reaches a certain age. That's something you will find out, no doubt.' She gave Rose a sharp look. 'Perhaps sooner rather than later.'

'*Mother.*'

'You can't blame me for being curious about the man who has wrought such a change in you. I don't think I've ever seen you looking so happy.'

Rose nodded. 'I'm not getting carried away but the fact is I like him. He's a good man, self-made. I admire that. I can't imagine his life has been easy and yet he is full of energy and optimism, someone determined to make the most of each moment.' She sighed. 'It's an outlook I very much admire and one that I happen to share.'

It went through Rose's mind that she was perhaps giving away too much too soon. After all, she had only been out with Harry once and she didn't know how he felt about her. No, that wasn't quite true. His feelings had been apparent in the way he had looked at her. He might as well have had them written across his forehead so obvious was the pleasure he got from being with her. She had received a card from him thanking her for her company. Another delivery of roses had arrived. The following week they were going to the theatre and Harry was fixing to have dinner at the Criterion with Lawrence Porter. Even though neither of them had said as much, Rose sensed their relationship had a future.

'All I've ever wanted is to see my children happy,' Martha said. She kept her gaze on the roses, where bees went from flower to flower. 'I was lucky, finding your father. Not everyone has such good fortune.'

'How long was it before you knew that he was the one for you?' Rose asked.

Martha turned to look at her. 'I knew at once. Not for a moment was there a shadow of doubt. It was the same for him. In my experience, it's a rare thing for true love, lasting love, to find you. It's something I gave thanks for every day I had with your father, and still do now. It's not a gift everyone receives.' She glanced at Rose. 'If it comes your way then you really are blessed.'

As her mother's words sank in Rose's thoughts turned to her father, a man she had few memories of. Much of what she thought she remembered she suspected had been told to her by others. She pictured a lean, tall figure, dark hair swept back, clad in sombre black and grey. She had no real memory of being held by him, the two of them laughing, although she did recall once seeing her father take her mother's hand and plant the most tender of kisses on it. They were at the dining table and Rose was peeping in through a crack in the door. From where she stood she could not see the look on her mother's face but her father was clearly visible, gazing at his wife with what Rose recognized as love. Love, and something else. As a child, Rose had not known what this 'other' thing was. Now, she would call it desire. Her parents had really loved one another. That her father had fallen ill and died was tragic.

'How do you know?' Rose said. 'I mean, when you meet the right person, how can you be sure?'

Martha took her daughter's hand in hers. 'Oh, darling, you know. You can feel it,' she said, echoing what Rose had said to Harry in the courtyard at the gallery a few nights before. 'Your heart tells you. Your gut, too. When someone lights a flame inside you, not only can you feel the glow but everybody else can see it. If I'm not mistaken, I can see that glow right now in you.' She paused. 'Then again, it could just be those Impressionist paintings making an almighty impression on you. Might be nothing to do with Mr Harry Gordon Selfridge …'

Rose laughed again. Suddenly, out of nowhere, she was gripped with fear that Harry might not feel the way she did. Despite intending to be discreet she had managed to tell her mother exactly what was going on inside her head – and her heart.

'What if I'm getting it all wrong?' she said. 'Here I am rushing headlong into something that might exist only in my fevered imagination.'

'That's the thing about love, dear. It's a risky business. You have to be willing to make that leap of faith and trust it will all work out for the best. Love can be as full of pain as pleasure.' She gave Rose a wry look. 'That's something you'll find out too. Your father used to be fond of saying every action has an equal and opposite reaction.' Rose gave her a curious look. 'I find it a comforting thought when things aren't going so well. I tell myself in time the opposite will happen. It became something I repeated to myself on very many occasions after your father died. The downside is that moments of intense joy will be countered too – not something you want to be thinking about right now, I imagine. It's life, though. Love, too. Ups and downs. Better than everything being flat and predictable and, I don't know – *samey* – don't you think?'

As Rose absorbed her mother's words she did not for a moment imagine they would very soon apply to her own circumstances.

11.

'I'm sorry if the play was a little on the dull side,' Harry told Rose as the curtain came down at the Auditorium Theatre.

He had managed to get excellent seats but the production of Ibsen's Ghosts, with its less than flattering portrayal of marriage, was perhaps not the wisest of choices. An hour or so in he had begun to worry that Rose would find the evils of marriage being depicted on stage off-putting. When he glanced at her, however, she seemed thoroughly absorbed.

She pulled on a pair of ivory gloves with shiny mother of pearl buttons. The leather was exceptional, so soft and fine it resembled satin. Harry leaned in for a closer look.

'May I?' he said, taking her hand and examining the glove. 'These are very beautiful. Did you find them here in Chicago?'

She shook her head. 'They came from Paris a year ago. I have another pair, almost a midnight blue with jet buttons. They're handmade. I found them in the Marais district.'

Harry made up his mind to track down the manufacturer and bring over as much stock as he would let him have for

Marshall Field. He could think of plenty of wealthy shoppers who would want something of such quality.

Rose took his arm and they descended the sweeping staircase from the dress circle to the lobby. The Auditorium had not been open long and was being hailed as one of the finest examples of architecture in Chicago. Harry found the scale – what for him was the swagger of the building – utterly breathtaking. It seemed to have risen up on the corner of South Michigan Avenue and Congress in no time, towering over its neighbours, demanding respect, crying out for attention. It was the kind of building that made a big bold statement. *Look at me*, it said. *Did you ever see anything so fine?* As Harry took in the grand surroundings, he was thinking, *One day, I'll build a store as impressive as this, a temple to shopping, and everyone who comes through the doors will be awestruck.*

As they made their way to the entrance where the carriages waited, Harry detected one or two pointed stares, a whispered remark here and there. It was clear to him he and Rose were the subject of gossip. He imagined the unease among the city's traditionalist elite at Miss Buckingham's dubious choice of company. He couldn't help smiling although at the same time he didn't like to think of Rose as the target of tittle-tattle. Again, he stole a look at her, noticing how she carried herself, head high, magnificent. If it bothered her what anyone else might think she certainly didn't show it. They stepped out into a mild clear night. The moon, almost full, sat heavy in the sky. An idea came to him.

'How would you like a stroll in Jackson Park before I take you home?' he said.

Rose's face lit up. 'That's right beside the Harper Lane development.'

Harry gave an enigmatic smile. 'I was thinking we could swing by there too and you could give me the guided tour.'

They got into the carriage and headed out of the city. Rose was animated, explaining what she had set out to achieve with Harper Lane, how it was much more than a housing development. It was, she told him, a community in its own right with shops and places for neighbours to meet and mingle. Harry, listened, letting her talk, not interrupting. The passion she felt was contagious and by the time they reached Harper Lane he was as excited about it as she was. They exited the carriage and Rose showed him the completed villas, some already occupied, some yet to be sold. The smaller houses, the ones she termed artists' cottages, were nearing completion and had a quaint charm about them, each with a touch that made them unique from their neighbours. Harry could see why Rose was so enthusiastic. In front of the block where the shops would go was an area marked out as a communal square with gardens. She was working with specialist fabricators, she said, to have ornate railings made, and inside intended to plant trees and colourful flowers.

'So, what do you think?' She said, pausing for breath at last.

Harry gazed about him. 'You're making your mark, Rose, putting something of yourself into what's going to be one of the best neighbourhoods in Chicago, that's what I think.'

He had a sudden desire to take her in his arms. In the moonlight she looked ethereal, a vision. They looked at each other for a moment and then Rose reached out and took his hands in hers. 'Thank you, Harry. Your opinion means so much to me.'

Again, he wanted to embrace her but held back, concerned it would be a step too far. Instead, he continued to gaze into her eyes until she laughed and looked away, shy all at once.

'What is it?' she said, looking up, finding his eyes still on her.

He wrestled with his feelings, not quite sure this was the moment to tell her how he felt, that he thought about her every day and when they were apart his mind raced with ideas about where he might take her. He dared not say he had imagined making her his wife for although he was sure of his own feelings he also had doubts that, despite the pleasure she seemed to take from being with him, Rose might not regard him as marriage material. The two of them stood on the sidewalk in the moonlight as the neighbourhood slept.

'It struck me,' he said, at last, 'that I have never met anyone quite like you, Rose Buckingham.'

12.

Every year in Chicago Clarissa Feldman held a Fourth of July ball at her sumptuous home on Lake Drive, regarded as the city's millionaires' row. She brought in an orchestra, caterers, a not-so-small army of waiting staff, and a seemingly endless supply of champagne. The first floor ballroom with its Italian crystal lamps and ceiling fresco was always filled to capacity. According to Clarissa, she issued invitations to six hundred guests and it was unheard of for anyone to turn her down.

Harry regarded Clarissa Feldman and her husband, Lincoln, as good friends. They were keen supporters of his. Lincoln had no problem with Harry coming from humble beginnings since the same applied to his wife. A shipping magnate, Lincoln Feldman had employed Clarissa as part of his secretarial team. Before long, she caught his eye and he arranged for her to be transferred to his office and handle his diary. When he announced that he was marrying her some of his peers were scandalized. At the Chicago Club he was taken aside and advised that Clarissa – lovely though she was – was not the 'right sort.' The fact she was a good twenty years younger than him brought forth protests from those within his circle of friends. It got back to him that Clarissa Wentworth, as she then was, was a gold digger. Lincoln Feldman didn't much care what anyone else thought. He knew his own mind and he definitely knew his heart. His marriage to Clarissa took place at the Basilica of Our Lady of Sorrows – another minor scandal since Lincoln was not a Catholic but his young bride was. Some thought he had lost his mind, yet for ten years he and Clarissa had been happy and had produced two boys and a girl. No one any longer spoke of their unsuitability as a couple.

Harry relaxed in their drawing room, having dined with them. He puffed on a good cigar. Lincoln and Clarissa always had the best of everything and were unfailingly generous, sharing their good fortune with their friends. Over a meal that had comprised five courses and as many wines, Harry had confided in them something of his feelings for Rose.

'Of course, I already knew you two had been stepping out together,' Clarissa said, a glint in her eye.

She had the palest blonde hair, large grey eyes and a wide smile. Without doubt, she was a head-turning beauty. In her late-thirties she still boasted a clear unlined complexion and a sweet, unspoiled temperament. Harry could appreciate why Lincoln had fallen in love with her.

He sent a plume of cigar smoke towards the ceiling. 'I would have been disappointed if you hadn't known, he said. 'I expect you to be properly informed on what's what in Chicago.'

'I pride myself on having a finger on the pulse.' She aimed a smile at her husband. 'Don't I, darling?'

'I can be out and about all day while Clarissa is at home doing something innocent like embroidery and when I come in *she* will tell *me* all the news.' He gave an indulgent shake of the head. 'You're extraordinary, my love. I sometimes think you have some kind of special power that means nothing gets past you.'

'People just seem to want to tell me their most intimate secrets – and everybody else's,' she said. 'I take it all with a pinch of salt. Unless it concerns someone I'm fond of, like you, Harry, and then I file it away for future reference.'

'It's no secret I've been seeing Rose,' he said. The fact she had been with him at the Monet opening some weeks before had been reported in both the *Chicago Tribune* and *Herald* newspapers.

'Well, I'm very pleased,' Clarissa said. 'Rosalie Buckingham is an interesting woman – ambitious, talented, good company.' She put her head on one side and studied Harry. 'Rather like you, I'd say.'

Harry tried to conceal his pleasure. 'You know I'm bringing her to the ball?'

'Then we shall meet her. It's about time you found someone you were serious about; someone who deserves you, Harry.' Clarissa glanced at her husband. 'That's what we think, don't we?'

Lincoln stretched his long legs towards the fire that burned in the hearth. There was no need for it since it was a warm evening but the Feldmans enjoyed having a fire lit. Sparks broke away from a log and escaped up the chimney. The room was their favourite, Chinese in style with screens and ornate silk drapes. On the mantelpiece were artefacts that Harry suspected were worth a fortune.

'I'm getting the feeling you're serious,' Lincoln said. 'You've got a real spring in your step. *More* of a spring in your step than usual, let's say.'

'I might need some advice,' Harry said, turning to Clarissa. 'It's Rose's birthday the day after your party and I want to get her something really special, something I can give her the moment the clock strikes midnight. I was thinking of jewellery but I'm going to have to choose carefully. '

He had seen enough of Rose to know that she already possessed the most exquisite jewellery, much of it family heirlooms, the value of which he could only guess at. It was not going to be easy to pick something that would stand out in that sort of crowd. In his heart, he knew she wasn't the kind of woman he needed to impress, yet he wanted to give her the best money could buy. It was not about showing off but his way of letting her know how special she was to him. If he was honest, he wanted to give her the world. Only one person knew the depth of his feelings and that was his mother, Lois. She had a way of knowing what was going on inside his head, often being able to tell him what he was thinking before he was even sure himself, and had seen the change in her son. Lois had met Rose, albeit briefly, over coffee at the store and had later declared Rose delightful: intelligent, spirited and warm.

'You and I are going to have to go shopping,' Clarissa said.

Harry beamed. 'There's nothing I like more.'

13.

Things were awkward between Rose and her sister. Anna had taken it badly when Rose ducked out of having dinner with Tyler Collins.

'I don't see why you're so upset,' Rose had said. 'You and Frank will have plenty to talk to him about. You really don't need me.'

'Three is an awkward number, as well you know,' was Anna's retort.

Rose responded with, 'Ask Mother, then.'

Anna had glared at her. 'What's all this about?' she said.

'I might have other plans.'

It wasn't true. All she planned to do was spend a quiet evening in her own company since Harry was going to be out of town on business.

'Either you have plans or you don't.'

'Never mind your tricky seating arrangements, it's awkward for me too,' she had told her. 'Don't you think I'm a little too old for you to be pushing me in the direction of someone you happen to think is eligible, with no regard for my feelings?'

Anna had sighed in exasperation and given up. Knowing how stubborn Rose could be, once she had made up her mind there'd be no changing it.

Since Tyler Collins' outburst at the exhibition, Rose had kept her dealings with him to a minimum. She was careful not to create an atmosphere – they still had to work together – but beyond that she made a point of keeping her distance. Every so often she would catch him looking at her, his face a study in remorse and self-reproach, and her resolve would threaten to cave in. Whenever this happened, she made an excuse to go out into the garden and take the air. Although she felt sorry for Tyler she was also wary of him. He was going to the ball Lincoln and Clarissa Feldman were throwing. Pretty much all of Chicago would be there. For Harry's sake, she could not risk another humiliating encounter.

The day before the Fourth of July ball, Rose arranged to go into the office later than usual. She had something pressing to do, a ritual that had become something of an annual pilgrimage. She had the carriage drop her on the corner of Cleverley and Bennett and walked the few yards to the entrance to Richardson Cemetery. It was a grey day, the sky heavy with cloud, the air muggy. She followed the road that ran through the centre of the cemetery, turning to her left at the boxy hedge that separated plots with simple headstones, or none at all, from those whose final resting places were marked by mausoleums watched over by figures hewn from stone and marble. Rose stopped in front of a grave with a weathered angel on top of a plinth. She laid the lilies she had brought at the angel's feet and stood in silence. She did not visit her father's grave as often perhaps as she felt she should and felt guilty that her mother was there each week. Anna made a point of going at least once a month. In the case of Rose the visits had dwindled to once a year around the time of her birthday. She glanced about her. In the far corner, two men shifted piles of wet brown earth in readiness for a burial. Rose looked away. She had been at her father's funeral but had no memory of it. Only four years old, she had been too young to take it in. Or perhaps she had erased it from her memory deliberately, not wanting to carry such a painful reminder of his loss. She missed him. Not as her mother did, granted, but still she felt his absence only too acutely. Now that she had met Harry she wished more than ever her father was still alive. She sensed that something momentous was happening to her and dared to think of love and commitment; something lasting. She allowed herself to consider that she and Harry were destined to share a future.

'Daddy, if you can hear me, watch over me, will you?' she said into the clammy air.

She pushed a strand of damp hair off her face. 'I've met someone,' she told the stone angel. 'I think you'd like him. He's a good man.' She nodded to herself, seeing Harry in her mind's eye. So confident and capable, yet vulnerable too. She had glimpsed the chinks in his emotional armour on more than one occasion, seen him struggle to find the right words and give up. She imagined it must be difficult when convention dictated that it was the man who took the lead and laid his feelings on the line first, at the risk of being turned down. Rose had gone out of her way to make things easier for him, hinting at her own feelings. She had given him all the encouragement she could without coming right out and telling him how she felt about him.

'I think I'm in love,' she said in barely a whisper.

After a minute or two she went back the way she had come and found her carriage waiting at the cemetery gates.

14.

While Rose was visiting her father's grave, Harry was in his office meeting with a journalist by the name of Drew Oliver. Oliver worked for the *Herald* and saw to it that the name of Marshall Field made regular appearances in the columns of his newspaper. He had pinned his colours to Harry's mast, recognizing an outstanding self-publicist when he saw one, and made a point of calling in at the store on a regular basis in search of a story. Harry never disappointed. He could drum up a good few column inches out of thin air. Every time a story ran suggesting that Marshall Field and the innovative Mr Selfridge were nudging ever further in front of the competition, the impact on trade was tangible.

On this occasion, Harry had fed Oliver the titbit of a craftsman in Paris, the only one of his kind, making the finest leather goods which he had agreed to supply only to Marshall Field in the United States. The fact Harry had yet to track down the glove maker in question, let alone do a deal with him, were minor details. He was confident of making it happen. *Believe and you will receive* was one of his mottoes.

Harry checked his pocket watch. Drew Oliver, sensing that their meeting was about to conclude, stuck his notebook in the pocket of his jacket.

'Shall I leave you in peace?' he said.

Harry seemed pensive and didn't answer straight away. He leaned forward, elbows on the desk, a pair of oval cufflinks visible at the cuff of his crisp white shirt. 'Can I ask you something, Drew?'

'Always at your service, Harry.'

'It's a personal matter, something private. It has to remain strictly between us. *Strictly.*'

Drew Oliver was intrigued. 'I give you my word. You can trust me, Harry, one hundred per cent.'

Harry gave a nod. 'My father left to fight in the war when I was five years old. I haven't seen him since.'

'I'm so sorry.'

'I remember very little about him and growing up not having him around, well, I just accepted it. I never really felt the need to know the details of what happened to him.' He hesitated.

'And now you find you're curious, is that it?'

He had a picture in his head of his father, a well-built man with jet black hair and an almost brooding intensity. Lois called him one of life's deep thinkers. Harry had his father's eyes. He only knew as much because Lois had told him. Lois had also told him that at times he was so like his father it was uncanny. If Harry was honest, the memory he carried around of the handsome figure in the dark blue dress coat, the blue pants with a stripe running down the outside seam of the leg, was probably put together based on what he had been told rather than anything he had seen. He could not recall his father saying goodbye and leaving to go to war, although, apparently, he had stood on the front step hand in hand with his mother and waved him off.

'There's a huge question mark in my head over what happened and I can't shake it. All I know for sure is that he's dead, not how or what happened. For reasons I can't even explain to you I want to find out. He died on the battlefield, but how? In all that went on during the fighting – what my mother terms the confusion of war-' Harry gave a helpless shrug – 'I guess the finer points of what became of him must have gotten lost. I need to know, Drew. Maybe it's getting older that's at the bottom of all this, thinking about the kind of father I'd make …' He left it at that, feeling he was in danger of giving too much away.

Neither of them said anything. Drew Oliver got up and walked over to the window overlooking State Street. Below, a city teeming with people, building on its prosperity, went about its business. It was nearly thirty years since the Civil War had ended and the chances of uncovering the story of a single casualty were slender. Still, Drew was a good investigator and he held Harry in high regard. He would see what he could do.

What went through Harry's mind was that it was no longer enough to explain away his absent father by saying he was a war hero. He wanted to know what Major Robert Selfridge's Civil War had been like; where he fought, what he went through. Above all, how he died. Harry would have children of his own one day, God willing, and it mattered that he would be able to tell them the truth about the grandfather they would never know.

'I can help, Harry,' Drew was saying, his notebook back out of his pocket. He sank back into the chair facing his friend and jotted something down. 'No promises, but I'll see what I can find out.'

Harry gave Drew the few sketchy details he had. The fact his father died on the battlefield in Pennsylvania, like so many others, probably didn't narrow things down much. More than twenty-five thousand men, many of them from the Union side, had died in the fighting there. It was a start, something to go on, at least. In the five years the conflict had lasted, more than 600,000 lives were lost. The scale of the losses was staggering, yet there were no burial records, no messengers despatched to tell families the fate of their loved-ones; no cemeteries for the fallen. Men like Robert Selfridge had gone to war and, quite simply, vanished.

It was beyond Harry's comprehension.

He knew only too well what lay at the root of his newfound need to know; Rose. Meeting her had made him take a long and searching look at himself. Who was he, really? The product of his parents, in essence. Everything he knew about his mother, a woman of such strength and spirit, told him that his father had to have been a special man. He had never before given any thought to the fact Lois didn't even have a grave to visit. She had never complained but now he could see how much heartache that in itself must have caused her. Harry was glad he had taken Drew into his confidence. Their conversation had given him some clarity right away. With luck, he might be able to fill in some of the gaps concerning his father.

It could only be a good thing.

15.

Rose spent the best part of the day getting ready for the Fourth of July ball at the Feldman mansion. She had decided well in advance what she was going to wear, a pale yellow dress in sheer silk chiffon. At the last minute she decided it was not right. Several dresses were now strewn across the bed and the chairs in her room. Daphne, the young girl who had been working for the Buckingham family for not quite a year and whose job it was to help Rose get ready, gazed about her, trying to remain calm while Rose paced the floor, getting herself into the kind of state Daphne's mother would have called 'a real tizzy.'

Rose came to a halt in the centre of the room, hands on hips, surveying the chaotic scene in front of her. She stood stiffly, her body full of tension. It seemed she had lost all power to make a decision, which was certainly not like her. Rose was known for her cool head under pressure, for her air of what many viewed as serenity. Why, then, was she unable to think clearly? And about a dress, for goodness sake. She really had to get a grip on her feelings or the entire evening would be a disaster. She thought about Harry, who had no doubt been hard at work in the store all day, managing crises, devising strategy, motivating the staff. If he could see her now in such a flap over her outfit she dreaded to think what he might think.

'Excuse me, Miss …' Daphne ventured.

Rose turned and saw the girl standing at the side of the bed holding up a dress in pearly white taffeta. It was a simple design, uncluttered, its skirt less full than Rose was used to. The dressmaker had said it was the new style that was coming in, what all the ladies in Paris were wearing. Rose loved it and yet had not yet felt confident about wearing it. It seemed a little too different. She did not particularly want to stand out so much from the crowd.

'All the dresses are lovely,' Daphne was saying, 'and you could carry off any of them.' She hesitated, as if unsure about going on. 'Of all of them, this one is special. I've never seen a dress like it, ever. If it was me going to the ball, well, this would be the dress I'd wear.'

Rose felt her shoulders relax. She tilted her head to one side and studied the dress. Daphne held it up in front of her. The girl was tall and slender with the same dark hair and pale complexion as Rose. The white gown did look good. It would definitely turn heads. Perhaps that was what was worrying her. She already knew she would get plenty of attention simply by virtue of being with Harry. Did she also want her 'forward' ball gown to be a source of chitchat? Again, she thought about Harry, his fearless approach to life, his willingness to take on Chicago's high and mighty, holding his own no matter what anyone might say or think about him. He refused to be cowed by anyone or anything. How hard it must be for him at times, she thought, and yet there she was, so self-absorbed that all she could think about was her outfit. A sense of shame washed over her. All this worrying was entirely unnecessary.

'I think you're right, Daphne,' she said. 'The white one is eminently suitable. Now we need to decide on the jewellery to go with it.'

Much was riding on this year's Feldman ball for Harry. It was the night when the whole of Chicago society would see that he and Rose were together. He felt it would add an air of credibility to the relationship, cement it somewhat. As for those who had something to say about the suitability of the match, well, he rather hoped their appearance as a couple at the most prestigious event in the social calendar would silence them once and for all. In past years, Harry had been accompanied by his mother. This year, she would be arriving with him and Rose. It felt to him as if that in itself held significance. He knew that Rose's mother would also be in attendance, that she was going with Anna and Frank. He gave a wry smile. The two families under one roof. He had yet to meet Rose's elder sister and brother-in-law. From what he could gather he had managed to work out that initially, at least, reservations had been expressed regarding Rose seeing Harry, and whilst Mrs Buckingham now seemed more accepting of the idea, he detected a lingering reluctance on the part of Anna. Not that Rose had said so in as many words. It was more what she didn't say when she spoke of her sister that gave things away. Harry was astute at reading between the lines

– even lines that were unspoken – and understood that Rose was warning him not to expect an enthusiastic reception from Anna. He smiled again. He was OK with that. It was what Rose felt that mattered.

As he waited for his mother to come downstairs and for the carriage to be brought round to the front of the house he reached inside his pocket and took out a small box in a velvet drawstring pouch. Rose's birthday present, chosen with the help of Clarissa Feldman. Harry had thought he knew the best jewellery designers in Chicago but Clarissa had taken him to a workshop he had never heard of where a genial man named Felton Noel was working with his two sons. Alongside more traditional pieces, the younger son, Peter, was doing what Clarissa described as experimental work. Everything was bespoke and unique, unusual. The young designer had wanted to know about Rose before suggesting something appropriate, nodding as Harry described the kind of woman she was. As soon as Peter Noel explained what he had in mind and sketched it out, Harry was sold on the idea. There hadn't been much time but the designer was confident he would have the piece ready for the ball. That morning when Harry had gone to collect it he had been overwhelmed by its beauty and the exceptional standard of the workmanship. Peter Noel, fresh-faced, sandy hair flopping onto his brow, had seemed overwhelmed too, given the generosity of the bonus Harry insisted he take for having completed the job at such short notice. Despite the young man's protests, it had seemed only fair to reward him properly for such fine work. Already, Harry's mind was turning over ideas, wondering if he could form a partnership with the Noel family, offering a bespoke service to the high-end spenders that shopped Marshall Field.

As Lois came into the room Harry slipped the pouch back inside his pocket.

16.

As the guests filed into the Feldman residence, Clarissa and Lincoln were there to welcome them. Waiters in black tie and tails, each holding a silver tray with glasses of champagne, lined up on either side of the room. On the stage at the far end, an orchestra played. The room was filled with flowers and overhead hundreds of balloons were suspended above netting, something Harry had not seen done before. He wasn't sure where Clarissa – for it was surely her idea – had got that one from. He moved forward in the line waiting to greet the hosts, Rose on one side, Lois on the other.

Rose looked extraordinary. Her dark hair shone and her pale skin was flawless, a shade or two lighter than the silk of her gown. He had never seen such a dress. It was almost conservative in its shape compared to the puffed-out skirts many of the women were wearing, and showed off her slender figure. At her throat she wore heavy necklaces of pearls in white, the palest of pink, and black, some of the strands almost reaching her waist. The effect was dramatic. Other than the pearls, she wore no other jewellery. Lois was traditionally attired in a dress of deep midnight blue. Harry, in tails and white tie, monogrammed gold cufflinks, felt proud to escort two such extraordinary women.

Clarissa's smile widened when she saw him approach. 'Harry, I am so pleased to see you – and with two beautiful women.'

He bent and kissed her hand. 'I don't think I need do any introductions. You already know my mother – and Miss Rose Buckingham, I think.'

Clarissa gave each of them a warm smile. 'You're all very welcome. I confess, there are people here this evening we barely know but Harry is considered one of our dearest friends.' Lincoln shook Harry by the hand. 'I hope this counts as a night off – no business talk,' Clarissa said.

Lincoln pulled a face. 'You know full well the wheels of commerce don't stop turning just because we're entertaining,' he said.

'I mean it,' Clarissa told him. 'It's a *party*. We expect you all to enjoy yourselves.' She turned to Rose. 'Your gown is quite ravishing. You must give me the number of your dressmaker. '

Rose smiled at the compliment. 'I will be sure to.'

'We'll have lunch one day.' She gave a playful glance in the direction of Harry. 'We can exchange information about this fascinating man.'

'Clarissa, dear, that's hardly fair,' Lois said.

'You must come too, of course.'

Harry held up his hands in surrender. 'Why is it I get the feeling odds are being stacked against me?'

'Nonsense. We're all on your side. While we're discussing your many qualities you can always dine at the club with Lincoln and chat about whatever it is you men find interesting – the export trade, perhaps, or what grain prices are doing to the economy-' she shot a look at her husband.

Lincoln rolled his eyes. 'I fear I'm still in the doghouse over a rather dull business discussion my wife was forced to endure over dinner a night or two ago.'

'It was the most tedious thing. I promise, if I ever hear another thing about wheat yields I will scream.'

Harry laughed. 'I think this might be a good moment for us to move on and leave you good people to greet the rest of your guests.' He gave Lincoln a look of sympathy. 'We'll see you later.'

Harry checked his pocket watch from time to time, keen to present Rose with her birthday gift on the stroke of midnight. The two of them strolled among the guests, greeting people they knew, each introducing the other to various friends and acquaintances. Harry was aware that Rose was drawing admiring looks from both men and women. She really was the belle of the ball. Shortly after arriving, they had encountered the rest of the Buckingham clan and the two matriarchs had met. It had seemed to go well. Anna, Rose's sister, had been cool but cordial towards Harry. In contrast, Frank, her husband, exuded warmth and good humour, talking with passion about the Harper Lane development. When Harry said he had visited with Rose and found it impressive he caught the look of surprise on Anna's face. Clearly, she knew nothing of the late-night moonlit stroll the pair had taken. Frank wanted to hear more about what Harry thought.

'I think what you've done there -' he glanced at Rose '-is truly innovative. You're ahead of the pack, I'd say, and that's something I like very much. I think you'll find others following your lead now.'

Frank had beamed with pride while Rose aimed a grateful smile at Harry. Anna might have chosen to act a little on the cool side but it was clear that Harry had won Frank over.

It was gone eleven thirty when Harry became separated from Rose. They were chatting with Clarissa when Lincoln appeared and said there was someone he wanted Harry to meet.

'I hope this isn't a business introduction,' Clarissa said, narrowing her eyes, placing a protective hand on Harry's shoulder.

From the look on Lincoln's face that was exactly what it was. 'I won't keep him more than five minutes, I promise.' he said. 'Titus Gray leaves town tomorrow and I don't want him to go without linking him up with Harry.'

Titus Gray, entrepreneur and philanthropist, was one of the wealthiest men in the United States.

'I forbid it,' Clarissa said, good-humouredly placing herself between her husband and Harry.

'He could be good for you,' Lincoln said, sidestepping his wife and leading his friend away.

Rose sipped at her champagne. 'It really is a lovely party. How do you manage to pull it all together? It must take months of planning.'

'There's no secret – I get other people to do it,' Clarissa said, laughing.

The sight of Tyler Collins approaching, champagne in hand, sent a tremor of anxiety through Rose.

'Mind if I join you?' Tyler positioned himself next to Clarissa, facing Rose. 'Thank you so much for a lovely evening, Mrs Feldman,' he said.

'Oh, it's far from over. We still have the balloons to pop.'

Tyler glanced up at the ceiling. 'I wondered what was happening there.'

'You'll find out soon enough. It all happens at midnight.'

Rose smiled, relieved that Tyler appeared sober.

'You look magnificent, by the way,' he said, his gaze lingering on Rose.

She looked away. 'Thank you.'

'We work together,' Tyler told Clarissa. 'I'm the architect on the Harper Lane development.'

Clarissa held up a hand to stop him. 'No shop talk, not tonight. It's a party.'

Where's Harry? Rose thought, her eyes searching the room. Tyler shifted to the side, blocking her view.

'Will you excuse me? I've just spotted someone I haven't caught up with in ages.' With that, Clarissa was gone, leaving Rose with Tyler.

Several seconds of silence stretched between them.

'Still seeing the mysterious Harry Selfridge, then?' He kept his tone light.

Rose stayed silent. She really could not bear another outburst. After a moment she said, 'There's no mystery to Harry. What you see is very much who he is.'

'I care about your happiness,' he said, his brow furrowed in concern. 'I don't want to see you hurt. I mean, how much do you know about him – really know?'

'I know he's too decent to cause any kind of scene or make me feel uncomfortable at a party.' She was defiant.

Tyler appeared chastened. 'I'm sorry, that's not my intention.'

'You've got him wrong,' Rose said. 'The more time I spend with him the more I get to see how kind he is – and how well thought of. The Feldmans, the people whose champagne and hospitality you are happily consuming-' she looked pointedly at his glass –'just happen to be close friends of his. If that's not a good recommendation, I don't know what is.'

Tyler raised an eyebrow. 'That's one way of putting it, I suppose.'

Rose looked about her again, wishing Harry would turn up and save her from what was becoming an awkward conversation.

'I suppose you know they're lovers,' Tyler said. 'Clarissa Feldman and Selfridge.'

He took a moment to study Rose's crestfallen face. 'You really didn't know, did you?'

She was reeling. 'That's absurd.'

'I'm so sorry, I thought you must have known. It's not exactly a secret.' Now Tyler looked uncomfortable. 'You must have noticed how often he takes business trips.' Rose said nothing. 'I hate to say this, Rose, but they're an excuse for nights spent at Chicago's various "houses" – or with Mrs Feldman.'

Rose felt sick. 'I can't imagine why you'd say such a wicked thing.'

Tyler was looking at her with what she took to be pity. 'I care about you. I don't enjoy seeing you made a fool of, that's why.' He sighed. 'Rosalie, you must have heard the gossip.'

She had and had chosen to dismiss it. She wanted to decide for herself.

'Didn't you see how close he and Mrs Feldman were?' Tyler said. 'Look, I know a good friend of the Feldmans, someone close to both of them. Lincoln Feldman turns a blind eye for the sake of his marriage and children.'

Rose felt as if the room was spinning. She could not speak.

'It was crass of me to mention any of this tonight. Forgive me.' He hesitated. 'It's just, I can't bear to see you shown so little respect.'

As the clock in the library chimed a quarter to the hour, Harry tried to make a move but Titus Gray was in the middle of a story about a business venture in London and it was impossible to get away. Lincoln was right about Gray. He was an extremely good connection. A big solid man with silver hair and green eyes he was easy company too, as good a listener as he was a raconteur. He seemed to take to Harry at once, perhaps because Lincoln had already paved the way for his friend. Under normal circumstances Harry would have been happy to sit and talk the night away but on this particular occasion his mind was on Rose. As the time crept towards midnight and a break in the conversation occurred he seized his chance.

'The last thing I want is to be rude,' he said, 'but I've left a young lady alone in the ballroom and if I don't get back to her I'm afraid she won't be too happy.'

'Then you must go,' Titus Gray told him. 'Scoot.'

'Good to meet you.'

'Look me up in New York. Or London, maybe. I'm spending a lot of time there these days.'

Harry mouthed a thank you at Lincoln as he slipped out of the room and made his way back to the ballroom, checking his watch as he went. Damn. It was after midnight. He felt in his pocket for the velvet pouch as he picked up his pace. He had been gone far longer than he intended. He only hoped that Clarissa had taken care of Rose for him. Rounding a bend in the passage he almost collided with a figure coming the other way.

'Clarissa!'

'Where's the fire, Harry?' she said, amused.

He frowned. 'I thought you were with Rose.'

'I was but a friend of hers joined us and then I saw one of my old friends so I left them chatting.'

'You don't happen to know who this friend was?'

Clarissa looked thoughtful. 'I didn't get his name but he said they worked together. I think he's something to do with her housing development.

Tyler Collins.

'I need to find her.'

'And I need to find my husband. If I catch him having anything remotely like a business meeting he'll be in the worst kind of trouble.'

Harry moved off, calling over his shoulder, 'He's in the library. And don't be too hard on him – he just did me the biggest favour hooking me up with Titus Gray.'

The scene in the ballroom was organized chaos. The balloons had been set free and were now all over the floor. Harry searched the room for Rose but couldn't see her. He made his way through the guests, asking anyone he knew if they had seen her. No one had. He went into each of the side chambers, gradually working his way to the end of the room occupied by the orchestra. Rose was the only woman wearing a white gown. She should be easy to spot. When he felt a hand on his arm he spun around, smiling, expecting to see her there, but it was Lois.

'Ma. You haven't seen Rose, have you?'

'She had to leave.'

Harry's face fell. 'Leave? Why?'

'She felt unwell. She said she had felt her head pounding for the last hour or so and could not bear it any longer. I sent her home in our carriage. I would have come to find you but she said you were in a meeting and not to disturb you.'

Rose had taken ill and he had not been there for her. The thought of her going home unaccompanied tore at him. 'She left alone?'

'Her mother went with her. Don't worry, son, she was in good hands. She said to thank you for this evening and that she very much enjoyed meeting your friends, especially Mrs Feldman.'

Harry's hand closed around the pouch he had been carrying all evening. His plan to be the first to wish her a happy birthday, to see the look on her face when she opened his present, lay in tatters. He had imagined it all, her happiness, the climax to a perfect evening, a memory for them both to cherish for ever. It had turned out to be nothing like that. He felt thoroughly deflated.

'When the carriage returns, I'd like to leave, Ma, if that's all right with you,' he said.

A few yards away, concealed by a pillar, Tyler Collins watched Harry's exchange with Lois. Whatever she had told him, the ensuing bewilderment and disappointment Harry felt was written on his face. Tyler did not know what had become of Rose after they had spoken. She had excused herself. He could see, however, that she was no longer in the ballroom. He allowed himself a smile. That little talk they'd had earlier seemed to have done the trick.

17.

The morning after the ball Rose felt like death, as if her head was breaking into several jagged pieces. She had barely slept and now the pain throbbing away in her temples was making her feel nauseous. The irony of her situation was not lost on her. When she had complained of feeling unwell the night before and left without saying goodbye to Harry she had not been telling the whole truth. It was not so much she had been *unwell* exactly as out of sorts and little wonder, given what Tyler Collins had told her. Harry and Clarissa Feldman. The revelation had been like a dagger in her side. She had known they were friendly – it was only too apparent from the warm way the two had greeted one another – but *lovers*? The idea had made her feel sick. How could he have paraded her in front of a woman who knew him intimately? Her head pounded. Clarissa must have been laughing inside at the ignorance of Rose. The woman had even invited her to lunch. With Lois. Had she no shame?

What made things worse in Rose's view was that Lincoln Feldman, clearly fond of Harry, counting him among his trusted friends, tolerated such an appalling betrayal. One so indiscreet it was the subject of gossip at the annual event the couple were famous all over Chicago for hosting. Callous beyond belief. Rose felt utterly humiliated. She had been wrong about Harry. Wrong on all counts. And now she was going to have to find a way of explaining why all of a sudden she no longer wished to see him. What a dreadful mess. She turned on her side and buried her face in the pillow. Tears streamed down her face.

When there was a knock at the bedroom door she ignored it. Another knock. Rose burrowed down and pulled the sheet over her head. The door opened.

'Can I bring you some breakfast, Miss?' Daphne hung back, half in, half out the room.

Rose emerged from under the sheet. The white dress lay across a chair, strings of pearls trailed on the floor. 'Can you please let my mother know I'm feeling no better this morning?' That was an understatement. She was, in fact, much worse. 'I'm going to have to stay in bed,' she said.

'I'll come back and put your things away. And, Miss – happy birthday to you.'

Her birthday. The last thing she felt like doing was celebrating. She was thirty years old and suddenly the thought of it made her feel depressed. Thirty years of age and alone with no prospect of marriage and a family. She had been foolish to allow herself to think that meeting Harry would change everything. Carried away by her feelings, she was now paying the price. It came to her that she had made an arrangement to see Harry later for dinner. She would have to cancel. Daphne hovered in the doorway, not sure it was all right to leave with her mistress looking so pale and distressed. Rose sat up, thanked her for the birthday wishes and grimaced. It hurt to move her head. Perhaps she really was ill, although she suspected the pain in her head was solely the result of her allowing herself to become so upset.

'See if you can bring me something for my headache, would you Daphne? I think my mother has some sort of concoction – a powder – that might help.'

Once Daphne had gone, Rose propped a pillow at her back. She pressed a hand against her brow. She would sit quietly and hope her head cleared. It was early, time enough for her to recover. What was she to do about Harry? She knew he was not the kind of man to be fobbed off without an explanation. Nor was he a man to have the wool pulled over his eyes. If she invented some story about not wanting to see him again he would see straight through it. She pictured that direct, penetrating gaze of his. It was part of the reason she had liked him. Harry was straightforward. Then again, how could he be if he was in a liaison with the wife of one of his closest friends?

She decided she would cancel their arrangements for later and allow some time to pass before telling him face to face exactly why she no longer wanted to spend time with him. The truth. He deserved it, even though it would be an excruciating meeting.

18.

In the wake of the Fourth of July ball, Harry was by no means his usual self, although on the surface he remained as ebullient and focused as ever. At work, he operated at his familiar hectic pace, razor sharp and in command of all that fell within his remit. He took to getting into the office earlier and earlier, drawing curious looks from the men in the loading bay. Within a week of the ball, he was behind his desk at such an ungodly hour he had to let himself in by a rarely used side entrance since no one else started work so early. Harry relished this time in the store. He paced about, scrutinizing the departments, the displays, the layout of the various counters. Every day he came up with a plan for making adjustments, some minor, some less so, with the aim of enhancing the shopping experience at Marshall Field.

In the evening, still buzzing with energy, he went out, often to one of the notorious 'houses' from which high class call girls operated, where he played cards into the early hours. The house he chose to frequent was George Manor, where the owner, Merilee Welsh, knew him well. It was understood that

Harry was not interested in the company of the girls and Merilee made sure he was not bothered. Harry had only ever come to George Manor to indulge his love of poker, despite what the gossipmongers might believe. In the space of a week, he arrived three nights in a row. He was, he said, on a winning streak, which was true. He was stacking up some impressive wins. All the same, Merilee Welsh was astute enough to know that something other than a desire for a poker game was drawing Harry to her establishment. She could see beyond the bravado and detected what she took to be an underlying sadness in his demeanour. She had gone so far as to ask what ailed him but he had brushed her off.

'Me?' he said, sounding breezy. 'I'm at the top of my game, Merilee.'

She backed off, even more convinced there was more to it than he was letting on.

Harry knew exactly why he was filling every waking moment. It was to take his mind off Rose. Just thinking about her and her sudden and inexplicable exit from his life was choking. Bad enough that she had left the ball without telling him – although he felt to blame for that for leaving her while he went to meet with Titus Gray – but since then it was as if she had retreated into a fortress that was off-limits to him. On her birthday, he expected he would see her, get a chance to give her the present he had so carefully chosen. They were having dinner together that night. All would be well. He had sent flowers with a note wishing her a good day and confirming what time he would call for her later.

A note had then arrived at the store for him. When he saw Rose's address on the envelope his heart soared yet once he read what she had to say he was disappointed. She regretted that she was still indisposed and would be unable to see him that evening, after all. She hoped that he understood. Once she had recovered she would be in touch again. *If you could please bear with me,* she had written. He read it several times, searching for the clues that lay behind the cool wording of the sparse few lines. The tone was formal. Not even a hint of affection. Most telling, no mention of the ball the previous evening, nothing to say she had enjoyed his company. Harry was no fool. Something was amiss, but what? He sensed that Rose was upset. Why, though? What had he done? Unless he saw her, looked into those amber eyes, and asked her directly, he had no way of knowing. He thought back to the ball, went through every detail up to the point at which Lincoln had taken him away for what was meant to be a few minutes. It had been fine until then, he would swear to it.

Now, sitting at his desk on the top floor of Marshall Field, he slid open a drawer and for the umpteenth time took out the note Rose had sent. Nothing further had come since then, although he had replied, of course. He had sent yet more flowers but when they brought no response he decided his attention was unwelcome. He took the jewellery from its box within the velvet pouch he had carried with him since the night of the ball. It seemed to have lost its lustre. He was no longer sure it was the perfect gift, after all. He sighed, replaced it in its box, tucked it back inside the pouch, and locked it in a compartment of his desk.

He got to his feet and went to the outer office where his secretary, Mary Walters, worked. He had a half hour to spare before his next meeting.

'Do you know Mr Donovan in the packing department – Danny Donovan?' he said.

'Yes, Mr Selfridge.'

'Would you mind having him come to see me please – soon as he can? Whatever he's busy with, ask him to leave it. I want to see him right away.'

19.

Rose felt bad for not seeing Harry on her birthday. Her headache had gone by mid-morning and she had no good reason not to go out for dinner that night, as arranged. To put him off by claiming to be unwell was dishonest and did not sit easily with her, especially when he responded with such kindness, sending yet more flowers in a box fastened with ribbon.

With the passing of a few days, she began to wonder if she was right to have reacted to what Tyler Collins had said in the way she did. Perhaps a more measured approach would have been wiser. Then again, it was nigh on impossible to be measured, given what she had learned.

Her mother had tried tackling her on the subject of her sudden change of heart towards Harry but Rose refused to say anything other than that she felt she had perhaps been too hasty in allowing her feelings to develop and needed time to gather her thoughts.

'A little time to think and reflect, that's all,' she said, playing down what she really felt.

Martha Buckingham saw right through that. Something was wrong, that much was obvious.

More than a week went by and Rose felt increasingly bad about her treatment of Harry. He had been unfailingly good to her and she had cast him aside without having the decency to tell him why. Whatever he had done, she still owed him an explanation. She made up her mind to speak to him.

Without telling anyone where she was going, she headed to Marshall Field, and made her way to the restaurant. It was early and only a few of the tables were occupied, although the one she had sat at previously was taken. The same young man who had served her before showed her to another one, closer to the entrance. From her vantage point she could see everyone who came in and, beyond, into the corridor that led to the fashion department. She ordered tea and settled down to wait, sure Harry would swing by. He had told her it was his habit to check on every inch of floor space during the course of the morning.

'Has Mr Selfridge been in today?' she asked, when the waiter brought her tea.

'Not today, Miss.'

Rose nodded, relieved. She had not missed him. She hoped that once he did appear Harry would join her for coffee and she would be able to talk to him, although exactly what she would say she was unsure. She wanted to see what her gut feeling was once he was sitting in front of her. And she wanted to be fair, give him a chance to put his side of things. She glanced about her. Perhaps this was too public a place for such a delicate matter. She strained to hear the conversations taking place at the other tables nearby and was unable to. It might be all right. Or, perhaps she could suggest they go to his office so that privacy was ensured. The last thing she felt like doing was causing embarrassment to either of them.

Time went by and Rose ordered more tea. As it approached midday she began to feel self-conscious. The restaurant was filling up with shoppers intending to have lunch. She could hardly hold onto a table over the restaurant's busiest period if all she was ordering was tea. Perhaps she should eat something. She was not in the mood. Where was Harry? At a quarter past twelve she gave up and left, thoroughly disappointed. It was her own fault, she thought, as she left the store without having browsed any of its goods, not in the frame of mind to shop; she could hardly expect him to show up on cue simply because she was now ready to see him.

In the carriage on the way home, she could not help feeling she had left it too late to clear the air.

20.

The *Herald* reporter, Drew Oliver, had news for Harry. He had made enquiries with a newspaper friend in Pennsylvania and unearthed some information regarding Major Robert Selfridge.

'There's no record of him having been killed,' Drew said. 'Which may mean he could well still be alive.'

Harry was taken aback. If his father turned out to be alive what could it mean – that he had chosen not to return to his family? The thought made him uncomfortable. 'There are no records for many of the casualties,' Harry said. 'The whole record-keeping side of things was a mess. I'm not sure that means anything very much.'

'I've got my man doing some more digging.' Drew caught the look on Harry's face. 'Don't worry, Thompson's discreet and we go way back. He won't breathe a word to anyone.'

'I hope not. I'm trusting you, Drew.'

'You can, I promise.'

Harry hoped he was doing the right thing. Secrets had a habit of getting out. It wasn't just himself he was thinking of.

It was his mother. Lois had no notion her son was digging up the past. What she would have to say Harry could only imagine.

'I've got a suggestion. Harry. Depending what Thompson comes up with I think it would make sense for you to take a trip to Pennsylvania.' As Harry seemed about to object Drew went on. 'Look at it this way, it can't hurt. At least you'll know as much as there is to know.'

'Which might not be very much.'

'Granted.' Drew studied Harry's expression. 'I can see you're cautious – and you're right to be. You don't know what you're getting into. For all you know, maybe you're letting the genie out of the bottle.' He waited a moment.' All I know is that if I was in your shoes I would want to find out whatever there is to know. Otherwise, in years to come, it may just gnaw away at you.'

Harry chewed it over. Drew had a point. Maybe he could bury his curiosity for now but the chances were it would just break back through into his consciousness in years to come.

'How about I come with you?' Drew said.

21.

'It feels like a while since we had dinner together,' Lois said.

'Sorry, Ma, it's just I've had a lot of business to attend to this past week or two,' Harry said. He cut into the beef on his plate exposing the pink inside of the meat.

Lois watched him acting as if the only thing he was concerned with was the food in front of him, knowing full well why he was being evasive with her; it was more than business that had been keeping him out all hours. 'This "business" wouldn't have anything to do with Rose, would it?' she said.

Harry put down his cutlery and gave her a wry smile. 'Anyone ever tell you being so sharp could lead to you cutting yourself?'

Lois frowned. 'What happened, Harry?' Her voice was gentle. 'The two of you were getting along so well and now … well, you don't even seem to be on speaking terms.'

'I don't think we are but I couldn't tell you why.' He pulled his shoulders back and aimed a bright smile at his mother. 'One of life's mysteries – what can you do?'

He's masking his pain, Lois thought. Pretending he doesn't care when it's plain he does.

'Why don't you tell me what happened.'

Harry laughed, a hollow humourless sound. 'If I knew, I would. The truth is Rose went cold on me and I haven't a clue why. Since she took off from the ball, sick, I haven't got near. It's like she's built a wall round herself.'

Lois was thoughtful for a moment. 'Maybe she hasn't yet recovered, then. There's some kind of summer complaint going around. Lots of people are down with it, not even able to get out of bed.'

Harry was shaking his head. 'Whatever happens to be wrong with her, it's not some summer complaint. She's out and about, only she doesn't want to see me.' He pushed his plate aside. So eaten up over Rose had he been that he had despatched Danny Donovan from the packing department of Marshall Field to Harper Lane in search of Rose. Danny had been given a spurious mission, instructed to say he had been informed by a friend of a friend in the building trade that Miss Buckingham was hiring labourers to work on the landscaping of the development. When he had arrived at the office asking for her, Rose had been nonplussed. There were no labouring jobs going, she said. She even apologized for his wasted journey and suggested where he might find casual work. When Danny reported back to Harry it was to say that Rose had, as far as he could ascertain, been in fine fettle. The fact she was at work when she had fobbed him off, claiming to be too ill to see him, had hurt more than he could ever explain. He felt embarrassed that someone he held in such high esteem would treat him so shabbily.

Harry glanced at Lois. He was not about to tell her what he had discovered. He was not about to tell anyone. 'With my hand on my heart I really have no idea what I've done to make her want nothing more to do with me.'

'I can't see that you've done anything.'

'I thought we were close, really close. All the signs were that she cared for me. You know how I felt about her.' Although he used the past tense, Harry's feelings for Rose had not gone away. 'And now … well, I don't know what to think.'

'You need to speak to her.'

'That's just it, she won't see me.'

'When was the last time you were in touch?'

'A few days after her birthday.' He had arranged for more flowers to be delivered with a card asking if he could call on her. Nothing had come back.

'I think you should give it another go.'

Harry shook his head. 'Oh no, I'm not lining myself up to get knocked flat again.'

Lois could see the hurt in his eyes. She hated to think he was getting his heart broken without even knowing why. Lois struggled with the idea that a sensitive soul like Rose could be capable of such cruelty. Harry deserved better.

'I know you've taken a knock and that the last thing you feel like doing is risking another but please don't let your pride get in the way of finding out what's really the cause of all this,' she said. 'You know what I think about pride. Holding onto it doesn't mean it'll make you happy. Or that you'll get the answers you need. What if Rose *is* ill but not in a way that shows on the outside?' She grasped her son's wrist. 'That's nothing more than a "what if?" by the way, but the point I'm trying to make is that you *have* to talk to her. Find out what's really on her mind. There's a chance you could put this right, whatever it is. Don't wait too long.'

When Harry said nothing, Lois added, 'If you're hurting this much I can promise you Rose is too. Go on, son – give her one last chance to explain. You may live to regret it if you don't.'

22.

The journey to Pittsburgh, Pennsylvania, had taken the best part of a day. In Harry's view, the railroad was not the most comfortable means of travel, on account of its constant shuddering motion, the clatter and clang as it thundered its way along the tracks. Impatient to get to his destination, he found he could not settle. While his companion, Drew Oliver, sat back and took in the passing scenery, Harry wandered along to the dining car and consumed enough coffee to wreck the chances of him getting much sleep later on. The cars rattled and shook, the view beyond the windows nothing but a blur. The day before, Drew had come to Harry with word that details had emerged of a Robert Oliver Selfridge, living in a suburb of Pittsburgh. According to Drew's buddy, Thompson, the man in question was the right sort of age – and was a veteran of the Civil War.

Harry had felt his heart beat quicken when Drew broke the news, even though he had tempered it with a warning they could be way off track and would only find out it was the right Robert Selfridge by going and seeing for themselves.

Harry wanted to know what Thompson had made of the man he had tracked down but it turned out he had not actually met him. 'All he got was an address,' Drew said. 'I told him to leave the rest to us. There's no point him going to see the fellow. It might scare him off if he thinks someone's trying to find him.'

Harry wanted to ask why someone making a few innocent enquiries would scare the man off – unless he had something to hide. He said nothing, since it had already crossed his mind that if his father *was* still alive and living just a few hundred miles away there might not be such an innocent explanation for him not coming home at the end of the conflict. He might well take off if he thought someone was about to find him.

Especially if that someone was his son.

Drew was right. From here on, it was up to them to find the final piece of the puzzle. All of a sudden Harry felt anxious. He had imagined finding his father would be a wonderful thing but what if it wasn't? He had a vision of his father shutting the door in his face. The Robert Selfridge he saw in his mind's eye was still dressed in the blue uniform of the Union army, a man in his thirties. He would be nearly seventy now. He thought about what might have happened to keep a man from returning home to his family after being at war. It was possible, he knew, that his father had suffered some sort of mental collapse, amnesia perhaps. What if he had no memory of Lois? Or Harry, come to that? What would be worse – his father staying away out of choice, or because his past life had been lost to him? Harry wasn't sure. He had felt a cold shiver at the back of his neck and knew he had to prepare himself for the likelihood of discovering some unpalatable truths.

He was grateful to Drew for going with him.

By the time the train arrived into Pittsburgh it was too late to go knocking on doors in a neighbourhood neither one of them was familiar with. Drew had wondered if they should get his friend Thompson to come along but Harry was reluctant. For now, all Thompson knew was that Drew was doing some research. He didn't yet know who it was for and Harry wanted to keep it that way. News had a habit of leaking out and, if it all came to nothing, he wanted to be sure Lois would never be any the wiser.

While Harry was half-inclined to take the address Drew had given him and go rushing out there, he knew it made sense to wait until morning. It was going to be disconcerting enough for whoever answered the door to find two strangers asking questions. From what Thompson had said, the Jonestown district was not the best in the city. Harry in his sharp suit and handmade shoes would cut an incongruous figure. At least in daylight he would seem less intimidating. They left the station and made their way to the Seventh Avenue Hotel, arranging to take an hour to freshen up and meet in the restaurant for dinner.

Once inside his room, Harry loosened his tie. He felt grubby from being on the train for so long and longed to bathe and change his clothes. The windows were open and a warm breeze made the sheer drapes billow. He looked around at the large, well-appointed room and a sense of despair engulfed him. For several minutes he sat on the edge of the bed and wondered why he was meddling in the past and what all this digging was likely to unearth. His mind was running on Rose too. His mother had been right; he did need answers. It was impossible for him to draw a veil over something that had been left hanging in mid-air. He had fallen for Rose and felt sure he had not misread her feelings for him. He put his head in his hands and searched for something, anything, to still the confusion he felt.

After a moment, he gave up. He needed to bathe or he would be late for dinner.

23.

The hotel arranged a carriage to take them to Jonestown, the clerk at the desk seeming surprised that two well-dressed gentlemen wanted to go to that part of town.

'Can I just check the address you've been given, Sir?' he said, concerned. 'Is it business premises you're visiting?'

'It's a private address,' Harry said. He had slept poorly – all that coffee on the journey down, no doubt – yet felt sharp and full of energy.

The clerk nodded, working hard to conceal his surprise. 'Would you like me to arrange for someone to accompany you, Sir?'

Harry exchanged a look with Drew. 'What for?'

'I'm just thinking it might be helpful to have someone on hand who can offer guidance, steer you through the neighbourhood. Those streets can be a bit of a maze if you don't know your way around.'

'You think we could use an escort?' Harry said.

'It wouldn't hurt, Sir.' He eyed the gold chain from the pocket watch in Harry's vest pocket, the chunky cufflinks. 'Better safe than sorry.'

As they waited at the hotel entrance for the carriage to come round, Harry said, 'What did you make of that? He looked at us like we're crazy wanting to go to that part of town.'

'It's a poor neighbourhood, not a bad one, as far as I know. Chances are we'll cause a stir, though.' Drew glanced at Harry, debonair, a gleaming top hat in his hand. 'I don't expect they're used to such-' he frowned, trying to come up with a suitable expression '*toffs* rolling into Jamestown.'

Harry had to laugh. '*Toffs*? It's not so long ago I was growing up in less-than-fashionable Ripon, Wisconsin. I haven't forgotten where I came from.'

Drew grinned. It was well-known that Harry Selfridge wore his humble beginnings like a badge of honour but this was the first time Drew had actually heard him talk about his past. 'Rags to riches, eh, Harry?' he said.

'No shame in that.'

'None whatsoever.'

The carriage came to a halt at the end of a street of properties that had clearly seen better days. One or two had boarded-up windows and peeling paintwork. At first glance, there was nothing to suggest Charlotte Street was unsafe, however. As Drew said, it was a poor area but not a bad one. They got out of the carriage and looked about, getting their bearings. The house they wanted was number 1157. A small boy in worn pants and a shirt too big for him emerged from a front yard and ran over. He stood in front of Harry looking at him as if he had landed from another planet.

'Don't suppose you can show us where to find 1157, Little Man?' Harry said.

The child blinked and stayed silent. Harry dug a coin from his pocket and offered it to the boy, who took it and ran back the way he had come.

'That worked,' Drew said, squinting in the sun.

'Let's just walk,' Harry said.

None of the houses seemed to have numbers. They were going to have to knock on doors. It could prove to be a long and tortuous process. Harry felt a tug at the back of his jacket and turned to see the child he had spoken to behind him. Without a word, the boy motioned to follow him and scampered off ahead.

'Guess we've found our guide,' Drew said, grinning, as they followed.

Charlotte Street stretched in front of them. After what Harry reckoned was nearly half a mile the boy stopped in front of a neat property with a well-tended front yard. Harry rewarded him with a few more coins and asked him to wait. The boy slumped onto the low wall that separated the front yard from the sidewalk.

On the porch, Harry hesitated before rapping on the door. This was the moment he might find his father. Or, he might just be in for a crushing disappointment. He swallowed. Drew placed a hand on his arm.

'Ready?'

Harry took a moment to compose himself. Did he want to do this? What if he came face to face with his father? How was he going to explain to Lois that he had gone behind her back? He glanced at Drew. They had come this far. His conversation from the other night with Lois when she had urged him to find the answers he sought where Rose was concerned came back to him. The same applied to his father. He let out a noisy sigh. He had to do this.

Raising his fist, he rapped at the door.

The woman who faced him on the porch was fifty or so with blonde hair going white woven into a loose plait that hung over one shoulder. She wiped her hands on an apron and gave her callers the same kind of look the boy had, as if they were creatures from another world. She pulled the door to behind her.

Harry gave her what he hoped was a warm smile. 'I hope we're at the right address,' he said. 'We're looking for 1157 Charlotte Street.'

She seemed unsure but nodded. 'That's the address. I can't say you're at the right place, though,' she said.

'Apologies for turning up without warning but I'm trying to find someone and this is the address I was given. I don't mean to alarm you but I didn't know what else to do.'

'I can't imagine there's anyone of interest to you in this house,' she said, taking a step back, about to go back inside and close the door.

Harry moved closer. He had not come all this way to have the door slammed on him before he had even got his father's name out. 'Robert Selfridge,' he said, the name tumbling out. 'Major Robert Selfridge. Does he live here?'

It was hard to read the woman's expression. She might have been nonplussed, suspicious or even alarmed. Harry tried to reassure her. 'Please, there's nothing to be concerned about. We're not here to cause trouble.'

'There's no one of that name living here,' she said.

'Maybe he moved on?' Drew suggested. 'Have you lived here long? He might have had the house before you.'

'I couldn't say. I can't help you, I'm sorry.' As she took a step back and opened the door a fraction further Harry caught a glimpse of something, movement, in the shadowy interior.

'Maybe someone else in the neighbourhood might be able to help. Please, it's important, we've come from Chicago,' Harry said.

She held his gaze for a moment. 'I'm sorry you've come so far. Really, I can't help.'

Harry pressed a card into her hand. 'If you run into anyone who knows him, I'd be grateful if you could ask them to get in touch. Please.' He had intended to leave it at that but, without planning to, found himself saying, 'It's a family matter. I'm begging you, please help if you can.'

On the far side of the street, leaning against the side of a sorry-looking house, a figure, his cap pulled low over his face, watched as the two smartly-dressed gentlemen made their way to a waiting carriage.

24.

It was three weeks since Rose had been into Marshall Field in the hope of seeing Harry. She had heard nothing from him, not since a few days after her birthday when the flowers arrived. She had not even had the courtesy to send a note of thanks.

At work, the final stage of Harper Lane was nearing completion. The remaining artists' cottages had gone up and were now in the process of being painted, their clapboard frontage given a pale yellow wash. The development still had a slightly unfinished look but once the landscape team got to work it would soon change.

With Harry out of her life, Rose realized how empty she felt. Before Harry, she had been content enough with her lot and had rarely hankered after a husband and children. Her take on all that had been somewhat philosophical; what is meant to be will happen, she had told herself. It was not as if she had a bad life. A lovely home, fulfilling work, money, the companionship of her mother. She frowned. Her mother, who so rarely enquired into matters regarding feelings, had been unusually forthright on the subject of Harry Selfridge's sudden disappearance. She was clearly perplexed that the man Rose had confessed she was falling for was, without notice, *persona non grata*. It was clear the situation made not an iota of sense to Martha Buckingham. Despite her mother's attempts to persuade Rose to open up, she had remained resolutely tight-lipped. She could not admit to a single soul what had put an end to her blossoming relationship with Harry. Of course, Anna had done her best to find out too but Rose refused to budge.

What she now knew about Harry she was not prepared to share.

She was alone in the office and sat at her desk sketching from memory a still life; the table in the restaurant at Marshall Field with its American Beauty rose, its china teapot and delicate cup and saucer, the soft golden light falling from the elaborate lamp onto the dark wood-panelled wall. She could picture it all with great clarity, each detail, down to the splashy design on the dainty cup and saucer. She would paint it, she decided. So lost was she in the sketch she did not notice when Tyler Collins came in. How long he had been standing behind her, observing as she worked away in charcoal she had no idea, but she had a sudden sense of being watched and jerked her head round to find him only a foot or so away. She felt the colour rise in her cheeks.

'Did no one tell you it's rude to creep up on someone?' she said, her voice sharp.

Tyler moved to the front of her desk. 'I'm sorry, I didn't mean to startle you. You were in a world of your own there. I didn't want to break your concentration.' He nodded at the sketch. 'It's good.'

She slid it from the desk and put it out of sight in a drawer. 'It's rough, not ready to be on show.' Rose gave him a pointed look, letting him know she was unhappy about him peering over her shoulder at something she considered private.

Tyler appeared contrite. 'I didn't mean to pry. It's just … well, I wish I could draw half as well.'

He was flattering her. Tyler's architectural drawings displayed a real gift. Her tone softened. 'You're being kind but I've seen your work and mine doesn't even come close.'

He opened his mouth to object but Rose put up a hand to silence him. 'You know I'm right.'

He laughed at the insistence in her voice. 'In that case, guess I'd better not argue.'

To her surprise, Rose found herself smiling. 'It would be wise not to.'

For once, Harry was not in the mood to dine out but since the invitation had come from his good friends, Lincoln and Clarissa Feldman, he was unwilling to let them down at short notice. That morning, at his regular meeting with Marshall Field, he had once again raised the subject of being made a partner in the store. Field was not unsympathetic. He valued Harry and was well aware his right-hand man could take his bright ideas and marketing strategies elsewhere and do very well for himself. Field understood why it mattered for Harry to be more than an employee – albeit a well-rewarded one. At the same time he was reluctant to hand over a slice of a business that had been in his family for generations. He gave his word that he would give Harry's proposal proper consideration, but warned it was not a decision he would make in haste.

As Harry dressed, knotting a tie in embossed jade silk at his throat, he went back over his meeting that morning. It was the second time he had raised the subject of a partnership and could see things from Marshall Field's point of view. If the business was Harry's would he want to give a chunk of it to an outsider? He might. Especially if the outsider in question was the employee responsible for raising the store to the top of its game.

Ideally, what Harry wanted was his own store where his initiatives paid dividends for him. It would happen, he was utterly certain. He dreamed of building a store people would marvel at, not just because the ethos would be shopping as pleasure, a form of entertainment, almost, but also because the building itself would be a landmark. The Auditorium in Chicago remained his inspiration. The man behind it, Ferdinand Peck, had dreamed of creating a theatre oozing grandeur on a jaw-dropping scale, and had seen his vision brought to life. His achievement resonated with Harry. Granted, the store he eventually built might be more modest, he thought, but, like the Auditorium, it would be the talk of the town. When it came to the store he would one day have he never for a moment considered it some far-off notion but an absolute reality. If he closed his eyes he could picture it as if it already existed. There was only one detail he was as yet unsure of and that was where it would be. Chicago or New York, most likely, but there was the whole world to consider. He smiled. In business, always aim high, he reminded himself. It was one of the many rules he observed in his daily life.

At his dressing table he opened a velvet-lined walnut box containing cufflinks, choosing a pair in white and yellow gold. He picked out a tie pin to match. As he put on his jacket, he went to stand in front of the full-length mirror at the far side of the room and studied his reflection, making a minor adjustment to his tie. The high shine on his patent leather shoes gave him some satisfaction. To the consternation of the Selfridge butler, Ralph, Harry insisted on polishing them himself since he was of the view that only he could get them looking so good.

Behind him, reflected in the mirror, was the four poster bed that had come from Paris, its heavy satin bedspread a rich ruby red. The drapes at the long sash windows were in the same jewel colour. For a while, he had allowed himself another dream, one that involved putting down new roots someplace else with Rose, the two of them making a home together. He felt the familiar wave of disappointment crash over him and straightened up, tugged at his cuffs. No sense crying over spilt milk, as his mother was so fond of saying.

No sense at all.

25.

'You've been a stranger these last few weeks.' Clarissa Feldman gave Harry an accusing look.

'No wonder – the poor man's run off his feet at that store of his,' Lincoln said.

That store of his. Harry wished. He sliced into the rib of beef on his plate, the meat soft and tender, falling off the bone. Hospitality at the Feldman residence was always impeccable.

'It's remiss of me not to make more time for my good friends,' Harry said. 'I hope you'll accept my apologies.'

'Of course,' Clarissa said. 'As long as you don't make a habit of it. We've missed you, haven't we, dear?'

Lincoln gave a nod. 'I could do with running through a couple of ideas with you, seeing what you think. You've a good nose for what's likely to fly and what isn't.'

Clarissa threw her hands up in despair. 'Please let's not turn a perfectly enjoyable evening into a business meeting.' She gave her husband a playful rap on the wrist and turned to Harry. 'I swear he intends to drive me insane, for ever cogitating on the dullest matters you can imagine.' Harry grinned. 'Then again, you probably find talk of enterprise and finance and heaven knows what endlessly fascinating.'

Harry waited a beat before answering. He noticed Lincoln gazing at his wife with undisguised adoration, Clarissa shooting him a conspiratorial little smile that let him know she was teasing, and something tugged at his heart. He so much wanted what they had and for a moment he really thought he had found it.

'In any case,' Clarissa continued, 'we're much more interested in hearing about Rose Buckingham.' She frowned. 'I have made efforts to arrange to meet, as we discussed at the ball, but it seems her diary is full to overflowing because of that wretched development of hers. I can see why the two of you get along so well,' she told Harry, her teasing turned on him now. 'You're exactly alike – work, work, work. It's a wonder you ever get to see one another.'

'Don't pry, darling,' Lincoln said, picking up on the look of discomfort on Harry's face.

'It's not prying when it's the welfare of one of your closest friends you're enquiring about,' she said.

Harry considered making a throwaway remark in the hope Clarissa would drop the subject. He didn't much feel like explaining what was going on with Rose. *Not* going on. Then again, why should he not tell the truth? They were his closest friends and he knew he could trust them not to gossip. If they were the ones suffering heartache he would want to know about it so the least he could do was be straight with them.

'I don't know what to tell you,' he began, glancing from Clarissa to Lincoln. Both had stopped eating. 'The truth is I haven't seen Rose for weeks. Not since the night of your ball, in fact.'

The moment he had uttered the words he felt better, lighter.

Clarissa was frowning. 'I don't understand, what happened?'

Harry shook his head. 'I don't understand either. The short answer is nothing happened. One minute we were having a good time, the next she was gone. She left without me.'

Clarissa was shocked. 'Not without telling you, surely?'

'She was feeling unwell, or so she said. It was while I was meeting with Titus Gray. By the time I got back to the ballroom she had already gone. My mother arranged for the carriage to take her home.'

'And since then?' Lincoln said.

Harry gave a shrug. Since then? Since then he had felt as if his heart had broken and was rattling about inside his chest causing him pain. Since then, his mind had raked over the coals of his relationship with Rose, searching in the ashes for clues to her sudden change of heart. Try as he may, he had not managed to come up with any answers that made the least bit of sense. It was obvious Rose no longer wanted to see him and he felt unable to press her for an explanation. Anything he now did would constitute unwanted attention. So many times, however, he had wanted to send her a card, flowers. He had received invitations and thought of asking if she would accompany him. Each time he was tempted to get in touch he had stopped himself. Right now she doesn't want to know, he told himself.

'The short answer is nothing,' Harry said. 'We had plans to meet and she cancelled. I wrote, enquiring after her health, sent flowers. I didn't hear back.'

'Then she must be ill, really ill,' Clarissa said. 'Harry, I saw the way she looked at you and how happy the two of you were. It was obvious she cared for you. She can't be well.'

Harry thought back to Danny Donovan going over to Harper Lane, finding Rose in apparent good health. Certainly well enough to be conducting business. He wasn't sure that telling the Feldmans he had effectively had Rose spied on would go down well but then again he had been desperate and it had seemed at the time the only way to get reliable news. He took a breath and explained, waiting for their censure.

Lincoln's face was a study in perplexity. 'Can't say I blame you,' he said. 'When someone vanishes from your life like that I think you've every right to do a little digging.'

Harry had been doing a lot of digging of late and not just where Rose was concerned. He had kept his trip to Pittsburgh quiet. No one knew the real reason for his visit. He decided not to say anything about that for the time being.

'I genuinely don't understand,' Clarissa was saying. 'The two of you are made for each other.'

'I thought so too,' Harry said.

'What are you going to do?'

He gave a wry smile. In business, if a plan didn't work out he was ruthless about dropping it, seeing what lessons were to be learned, and moving on. Take the hit and get over it, he was fond of saying.

The same would have to apply to his feelings for Rose.

26.

Harry was walking the floor of the store, greeting customers, turning over an idea in his head about giving the counter selling ladies' accessories more prominence. He might swap around handkerchiefs with gloves, freshen things up. The store was busy and trade appeared brisk. The warm weather had sparked renewed interest in parasols. Marshall Field had the best selection in the city, including a paper variety hand-painted to look as if they had come from some Far Eastern outpost. In fact, Harry had found a manufacturer of a rather ordinary range on the east coast of the US and persuaded him to jazz them up a bit. The resulting brightly-coloured parasols had been seized upon by the display team and were now dotted throughout the store, several suspended from the ceiling like exotic birds in flight. Needless to say, this exclusive range was proving popular with Chicago's society ladies.

'Perhaps you could advise on a purchase,' a voice from behind said, causing Harry to turn and find Tyler Collins approaching. Harry stiffened. 'I'm looking for something for a lady and, frankly, I'm finding the choice overwhelming. I had no idea there were such treasures to be had in a department store.'

'I'm confident any one of the staff will be able to assist you,' Harry said, beginning to move off.

'Oh, but I'm looking for something special – *for* someone rather special.' Tyler Collins smiled.

Harry remained polite. 'You won't be disappointed then. The store is full of special items, although-' he was unable to resist making a dig – 'the *really* special items might be beyond your budget. If you'll excuse me, I have a meeting.' He had barely begun to walk away when Collins called after him.

'Shame. Since you know the lady in question I was rather hoping you'd be able to offer some assistance. It's Rosalie Buckingham I'm buying for.'

Harry turned and gave Tyler a sharp look. 'It would be a pleasure to help you,' he said, keeping his tone pleasant. 'Since I haven't seen Miss Buckingham in the longest while, however, I'm really in no position to know much about her taste in anything.' He looked Collins up and down as if to say her taste in gentleman certainly appeared dubious. 'Now, if you'll excuse me, I've someone important coming in to see me.' Harry's emphasis on the word important seemed to hit home and the smile vanished from Collins' face. Harry checked his watch, aimed a dazzling smile at his rival, and departed.

On the management floor, striding along the corridor to his office, Harry gave instructions for his next appointment to be delayed by half an hour. He needed to clear his head before seeing anyone. Once in his office, he slumped in his chair, beset by a mixture of anger and disappointment tinged with humiliation. Harry was in no doubt that Tyler Collins had come to the store in the hope of running into him for the express purpose of letting him know he was the man in Rose's life now. He had wanted to rub Harry's nose in it. That was what the exchange on the shop floor had been about. Harry's elbows were on his desk, his chin resting on his hands. How could Rose be interested in a man like Collins? An individual who was low and undignified; the kind who, were he in the boxing ring, would hit his opponent below the belt. The encounter had left Harry feeling soiled and grubby. He would change his shirt before his meeting. Seeing Collins had thrown him right back into the confusion he had wrestled with over Rose's behaviour towards him. He had thought he was doing a good job of burying those feelings. To lose her had been bad enough but to think she had turned from him to a man like Tyler Collins made the situation even worse. Before he knew it he was once more trying to fathom why Rose had treated him so shabbily, stirring up questions about the kind of man he must be to invite such behaviour. A brief flurry of dark thoughts swirled about inside his head until he forced himself to push them away. *Pulling yourself to pieces won't help*, he told himself. *Plenty others willing to do that already, without you joining in.*

He thought back to the evening of the Fourth of July ball when things had somehow gone wrong with Rose. Clarissa Feldman had left her in the company of Tyler Collins while Harry was in his meeting. Clarissa detected nothing about Rose that suggested she was about to become unwell. Harry pondered. In the space of twenty minutes or so Rose had gone from being radiant to becoming so sick she had been forced to rush away. Harry sifted through his memories of the night, bringing to mind his meticulous search of the ballroom for Rose prior to finding out she had already gone. Images from the evening formed in his mind's eye as a series of moving pictures. He frowned. Come to think of it, following his meeting, he could not remember seeing Tyler Collins either. A poisonous thought burrowed its way under his skin. Had Rose left the ball with him? No, not possible. Her mother had accompanied her. Still, something was eating away at him. He began to feel sure Collins had been instrumental in her decision to leave early. Perhaps the two of them had history, which would explain his drunken outburst at the Monet opening. Perhaps Rose had been using Harry all along to make Collins jealous.

A knock came at the door. He glanced at the clock. His half hour was up. 'Come in.'

Drew Oliver stepped into the office and Harry rose to greet him.

'Brought you today's edition of the *Herald*,' Drew said, placing the newspaper on the desk. 'The interview about shopping and its place alongside cultural and leisure pursuits. It's rather good. If I do say so myself.'

Harry grinned and spread the paper out. The story took up most of page three. It might just be the nudge Marshall Field needed to finally agree to a partnership. 'Nice job, Drew, thank you.'

'Not hard to turn out a good piece when you're providing the copy, Harry. It practically writes itself.'

'We'll have dinner. My way of saying thank you.'

Drew smiled. 'Any more thoughts on Pittsburgh?'

He shrugged.

'I sometimes find when I'm chasing a story that the first foray yields nothing. Reporter turns up on the doorstep, everyone clams up, I go away disappointed.' Drew gave Harry a look. 'A bit like us showing up at 1157 Charlotte Street.'

'It was either the wrong house or the Robert Selfridge who lived there was long gone.'

Drew looked thoughtful. He pushed a lock of blond hair off his brow. 'Hmm … maybe. What I'm thinking is that the lady of the house might have known more than she cared to say. After all, we could have been anyone – debt collectors, rogues, racketeers-'

Harry guffawed. 'If I look anything like a debt collector, a rogue, or a racketeer, shoot me now.'

'Probably not the best examples. What I mean is that two outsiders showing up like that, woman on her own – even if she does know something, odds are she won't share it with a pair of strangers.'

Harry thought about it. 'I guess not. I did give her a card, remember, and made it pretty clear it was important. '

'All the same, we put her on the spot and maybe now she's had time to think she might be more talkative. Which is why I think we should make another trip to Pittsburgh.'

Harry thought about the railroad journey and groaned.

'Only this time,' Drew went on, 'we give the poor woman some warning.' Harry gave him a questioning look. 'Get my chap, Thompson, to go along first and prime her. My feeling is she'll be more inclined to look favourably on him than she was on us.'

'Another *rogue* at the front door? I can't imagine why.'

Drew smiled. 'Let's just say Thompson will be a lot less out of place in that neighbourhood than we were. He favours a – how shall I put it? – down at heel look. Finds it helps him gain access to the less salubrious parts of town.'

Harry sighed. 'I don't know. I was just coming round to the idea of letting the whole thing lie.'

So far, his efforts to trace his father had been low key. He had caused no upset, only to himself by awakening old feelings. Lois was oblivious to what he had been doing and he wanted to keep it that way. He felt bad about going behind her back. Even though there was much in his life he didn't share with his mother, mostly it was to do with business. If she thought he was searching for his father and deliberately keeping her in the dark about it, she would be so hurt. He wasn't sure he would ever manage to explain himself in a way that made sense to her.

'I don't know,' he said again.

'At least think about it,' Drew said.

27.

The next time Harry saw Rose was at a concert at the Central Music Hall. During the drinks reception ahead of the performance he caught sight of a woman in a pale yellow gown, standing with her back to him in the far corner of the room, and knew at once it was her. Some kind of sixth sense must have alerted her to his gaze because she turned and looked right at him. For a moment they gazed at each other before she eventually cast her eyes downwards and turned back to whoever it was she was with. From where he was standing, Harry could not quite make out her companion. Lois was at his side and witnessed the exchange.

'Son, speak to her,' she said.

Harry kept his eyes on Rose a moment longer. Taking a step to one side he saw she was with Tyler Collins. Harry turned away. 'I don't think that would be such a good idea, Ma.'

The concert went by in a blur. Harry barely heard the Boston Symphony Orchestra as it worked its way through pieces by Tchaikovsky, Brahms and Beethoven. He took his cue from Lois, applauding whenever she did. Rose was somewhere in the hall, in the company of Tyler Collins, and that was all Harry could think about. He was beginning to think his suspicions about the two of them being involved long before Harry even met her had to be true. He felt used. The same sense of being soiled that followed his bumping into Collins in the store once again took hold. Even at a distance, he found the presence of the man odious. He was poison and there he was, escorting Rose. It was not like Harry to get someone so very badly wrong and yet where Rose was concerned his usual good judgment had failed him catastrophically. He endured the concert in a state of deep gloom, not realizing it was over until Lois tapped at his arm to ask if he was ready to leave. Half the auditorium had already emptied.

'You've been in a world of your own tonight,' Lois said, in the carriage on the way home.

'I'm sorry to be such poor company,' he said. 'No excuse, it was rude of me.'

'I could see your mind was elsewhere.'

'There's a lot going on at the store.' He glanced at her. 'And I may have to make another trip to Pittsburgh, check that a new supplier is working out.'

'I don't suppose it was store business that stopped you enjoying this evening's programme.'

Harry said nothing.

'Harry, son, I know you better than anyone. Work doesn't make you distracted and out of sorts, quite the opposite. The busier you are, the happier. It was seeing Rose that brought

131

your night crashing down. I could see it in your face the second you clapped eyes on her.'

'The fellow she was with, Collins-' Harry shook his head wondering how to say what he had to and keep it polite. 'He came in the store and sought me out, just so he could let me know he was shopping for a gift for Rose.'

Harry recalled the way Collins had looked at him when he asked for advice. The sarcasm in his tone. He had come to Marshall Field with the sole intention of goading Harry, it seemed.

'Do you think they're together?'

'I think perhaps they were together the whole time.'

In the shadows of the carriage Harry made out the frown that appeared on his mother's face. 'That can't be true. She would never have introduced you to her family.'

'Unless she was looking to make him jealous.'

Lois thought about it. 'I can't believe it of her.'

'I hate the thought as well but I can't help wondering if the whole time she was playing me for a fool.'

The following morning after Harry had walked the shop floor he called in at the restaurant for coffee where he got into conversation with a pair of elderly ladies concerned that they had been unable to find a particular type of fur-trimmed leather glove. Harry spent several minutes gathering precise details of the gloves which, it seemed, the ladies had been purchasing at Marshall Field for more years than they cared to remember, and promised to source new stock.

'I suppose you have more on your mind than gloves, Mr Selfridge,' the taller and more sprightly of the two remarked.

'Not at all,' he said. 'At Marshall Field, the customer is always right. If those are the gloves you like I will do everything in my power to get them into the store for you. I happen to believe that in business you give the lady what she wants.'

The women gave him bright smiles. They exchanged a pleased look. 'On that basis, Mr Selfridge, you will not go wrong,' said the shorter one.

His black mood of the previous night had gone. He chose the table nearest the door and worked his way through two pots of coffee. As he was about to leave Clayton Francis, the waiter who had served him, asked if he might have a word.

'I don't know if it's important, Sir,' he began, 'but a lady was asking after you the other week. I'm sorry, it went clear out of my mind. It was only seeing you this morning jogged my memory. She was sitting at the same table.'

'It's OK, Mr Francis. Who was it – one of our regular customers?'

He shook his head. 'She didn't leave her name or ask for a message to be passed on or anything, merely enquired as to whether you had been in.'

Harry nodded, thinking it couldn't have been anything important. 'Don't worry, it can't have been urgent.'

'She was here a long while, as if she was waiting. I remember her looking up every time someone came in. It was only when people started arriving for lunch that she left.'

Harry nodded. 'Don't be concerned.'

'Only, I'd seen her before – with you. At the table in the far corner.'

Rose.

'When exactly was this?'

'I can't quite remember.' His brow creased in concentration. Something came to him. 'I do remember, there was a meeting that day, first thing, before we opened. The display team running through ideas for something they wanted to set up in the corridor between the entrance to the restaurant and the shop floor. So, the Fourth of July material must have been taken down by then.'

'Thank you, Mr Francis, you've been a great help.'

Harry asked his secretary, Mary, to speak to Cecil Crisp and get a date for that display team meeting in the restaurant. When she came back with it Harry realized that Rose had been into the store asking for him the week after the ball. It struck him he had mentioned calling at the restaurant for coffee every day and guessed she would have expected him to appear. He pictured her waiting until it became apparent he would not show up and his heart sank. If only she had asked someone to get a message to him. If only he had stuck to his usual routine that day. Frustrated, he pushed the thought away, knowing that to feel regret about something he had been oblivious to was utterly pointless.

The whole business was perplexing. That Rose had come looking for him a few days after receiving the last note he sent sparked a small glimmer of hope. She had not then turned her back on him, as he had thought, but had sought him out with the intention of talking face to face. That had to mean something. She had not made an effort to contact him since, however, which was less encouraging. Maybe that indicated a change of heart. Or that she had lost her nerve. Or simply felt that too much time had elapsed. Perhaps she believed word must have reached Harry that she had been there enquiring about him. If that was the case, she no doubt felt it wise to keep away when he had not subsequently been in touch.

His head was spinning with all the *ifs* and *maybes* jostling for position. Those, too, were pointless. There was no sense speculating. He should have listened to Lois when she told him the only way to work out was going on in Rose's head was to talk to her. It was one piece of advice he wished he had taken.

Now, having discovered that things weren't quite as he had imagined them to be, he was going to have to work out his next move.

28.

Harry was quiet during breakfast. Distracted. Lois ate only a small amount of what was on her plate, stealing a look now and then at her son, waiting for the right moment to break into his thoughts.

'It can help, you know,' she said, finally.

Harry looked up, puzzled.

'To talk about whatever it is that's on your mind.'

He pushed his breakfast aside. He had hardly touched it. Reaching for the coffee pot, he filled his mother's cup, overfilled his own, slopping some in the saucer, and sat back in his chair.

'I was thinking about the store,' he said.

It was partly true. Later, he would sit down with Marshall Field and press him for a decision on the partnership. Enough time had passed for his employer to have given proper consideration to his proposal. Marshall Field was a fair man, straightforward, yet Harry felt nervous. Despite telling himself there was no good reason for Field to turn him down he could not get rid of the anxious feeling in the pit of his stomach.

Based on all that Harry had done for the store he had proved himself worthy of a slice of the business, of that he had no doubt. And yet the tight feeling in his gut indicated that things would not go his way. He attempted a reassuring smile. Lois did not need to hear about any of this, not yet.

'I've an important meeting this afternoon, that's all it is.'

She was not convinced. He had important meetings every day of the week. She knew there had to be something special about this one. In the past, on big occasions, Harry had used her as his sounding board, had her listen to whatever it was he planned to say to make sure it came out right. She had one last shot at persuading him to open up.

'If there's anything you want to run past me before you head in, I'm only too happy to listen.'

He drank down his coffee and got up. 'Thanks, Ma, but I've already done the groundwork. Today is about seeing if it paid off.'

Once he had gone, Lois set aside her plate. She had made a good show of eating but, in fact, had hardly touched her food. She closed her eyes and allowed her shoulders to sag. She had felt off-colour for days now and done her best to ignore it. No matter how well she slept she had little energy when morning came. Getting up, dressing and breakfasting with Harry was as much as she could manage before a great tiredness overtook her. Perhaps it was simply that she was getting old, although she had a sense there was more to it than that. She folded her napkin and rested it on the table, picked up the newspaper. No good. She could not concentrate. She decided to retire to her room for an hour or so in the hope she would then feel somewhat restored.

On the carriage ride to work Harry was preoccupied with more than the store. Rose was also on his mind. She had come looking for him, but why? He didn't need to run that one past Lois to know what she would say. *Ask her*, would be his mother's response. He was not so sure he could now. Perhaps the moment for talking had passed. Rose at the concert in the company of Tyler Collins came to mind. She seemed to have wasted no time in moving on. He gave a wry smile, strongly suspecting past history between the two of them and at the same time not wanting to think that what he had with Rose was less than he had believed it to be. *Ask her*. Perhaps he should. At least then he would know for sure. One thing he could never stand was leaving matters unresolved.

His mind turned to Pittsburgh. He had come to a decision. What Drew had said made sense. If he put himself in the shoes of the woman on Charlotte Street, opening her door to two strangers, he could see it had to have been unsettling. Much as he hated the idea of another of those railroad trips, it was worth paying a second visit. One last attempt, he told himself. If there is even the slightest possibility it may bring me closer to finding my father then it has to be worthwhile. Meanwhile, Thompson would do what he could to put the woman's mind at ease. Harry thought back to standing on the porch of the house, the look of wariness in the woman's pale blue eyes. Her face told the story of a life that had not been easy. The shadow of something in the hall behind her came back to him. It had been so fleeting he could not be sure it was simply his eyes playing tricks. Now, though, he wondered if the reason for the woman's anxiety was that she had something to hide. Had his father been inside? No, he did not believe it. Not unless Robert Selfridge's mind had been so broken by war he no longer knew himself. Harry swept aside the uncomfortable thought that he might yet find his father only to discover he did not know the son who had come looking for him.

The carriage moved along State Street and came to a halt at one end of Marshall Field. Harry emerged into bright sunshine. Only a few wisps of cloud trailed across the blue sky. He walked the length of the store, checking the window displays, feeling a sense of pride. No other store in the city had such striking windows. He made a mental note to congratulate Cecil Crisp and his team. In the few minutes it took him to stroll along the block he could feel the heat of the city on him like a weight, clinging to his clothes, making his collar feel a fraction too tight. It had been a long, hot summer. He made his way inside where the temperature was a good deal cooler.

Rose sat at the writing bureau in her bedroom, In front of her was the walnut inlaid box where she kept cards and mementoes. She removed the lid and took out an envelope, blank, except for the date; July 5, 1890. The day after the Feldman ball. Rose's thirtieth birthday. Inside, were pressed flowers, the petals still a vibrant shade of crimson. Despite what she had learned about Harry, she had chosen to keep some of the flowers he had sent her. If anyone had asked her why she was not sure she could have explained. Sentimentality, perhaps. A wish to hold onto the memory of something all too fleeting yet precious. The sight of the flowers preserved in their state of partial decay made her reflect once more on how things had ended with Harry. Had she been too hasty? Too harsh? With the passing of time she could see that her actions had been unfair. Her parents had raised her to be open and understanding, to give people a fair hearing. And yet she had been quick to form a judgement without giving Harry any opportunity to explain. She felt the heat rise in her cheeks. Not that he could have offered any adequate explanation for his involvement with the wife of one of his friends. Right under Rose's nose, too. A thought wormed its way into her consciousness. What if it wasn't true? She thought back to Tyler's expression when he broke the news. He was not a bad person. She knew how he felt about her – and his disdain for Harry – but surely he would never stoop so low as to blacken a man's character unless he was entirely sure of his facts. She picked up one of the flattened flowers. Its outline, a faint red stain, remained on the paper. It was no good tormenting herself like this. A series of soft taps on the door made her jump. Daphne, her maid, came into the room. Rose pushed the flowers back inside the envelope, and tucked them out of sight.

'There's someone here to see you, Miss Buckingham,' Daphne said.

Rose felt a stab of hope. Harry. She got up and checked her reflection in the mirror, feeling her composure slip.

'I'm not expecting anyone,' she said.

Daphne handed her a calling card. Clarissa Feldman. Rose experienced a sense of disappointment mingled with curiosity.

For a second or two she had allowed herself to believe that just by thinking about Harry she had somehow conjured him up, yet she knew he would not call on her again – could not – not after the way she had treated him.

'Mrs Feldman is waiting in the drawing room,' Daphne said, sounding unsure of herself for having admitted an unexpected visitor. 'She said it was important.'

Rose nodded. 'That's all right, Daphne. Would you please arrange for us to have some coffee and let Mrs Feldman know I will be with her shortly.'

Rose took a few moments to compose herself. She was nervous at the prospect of confronting Harry's lover and had no idea what to say to her. It struck her that Clarissa Feldman had to be downright brazen to turn up like this with no prior warning. Then again, at the ball Clarissa had suggested having lunch with Rose *and* Lois Selfridge, a clear indication that the woman had no shame. Rose smoothed the front of her dress. In the mirror she noticed her skin was pale and that she lacked any sense of sparkle. When she was seeing Harry she had looked so different. Even her sister had commented on how well and full of life she appeared. The Harry Selfridge effect, Rose thought, filled with a sudden sense of longing to be back within that bright, high-energy orbit. She sighed. *You really did rub off on me, Harry*, she said to herself, before heading downstairs to face Clarissa Feldman.

29.

Lois decided to lie down. The tiredness she felt was overwhelming, as if something was pressing hard on her. She had experienced nothing like it before. Perhaps she was coming down with something and should call for the doctor. She did not want to make a fuss if all she needed was rest. Reluctant to spend too long lying on her bed, she asked that someone knock on her door in an hour's time – not that she felt it likely she would actually sleep.

As soon as she lay down, Lois felt the last remnants of her energy drain away. She must have contracted some illness. There was no other explanation for feeling so dreadful. A tremor of panic went through her. She was helpless and realized at that moment she could not have summoned assistance had she needed it. Her limbs were leaden. She made an effort to raise her arms off the bed and found it impossible. Fear replaced the panic. She stared at the plasterwork in the centre of the ceiling, the detail going in and out of focus. She blinked, raised her head off the pillow a fraction and focused her attention on the cornice above the window opposite. It too seemed uneven, not quite solid. The effort of staring at it became too much and she sank back down. Her head felt too heavy for her neck to support it. She had been ill once before, many years earlier, with something that had kept her in bed for a couple of weeks. The doctor had not managed to put a name to it but it had passed and in time she had got back her strength. This time was different. There was a fuzziness at the back of her eyes, a sense that she was not quite in control of her movements. Fear flared inside her once more. She thought about Harry and wished she had said something to him at breakfast, at least hinted that she was not quite herself. She should not have let him go off without a word. Her throat felt dry. A pitcher of water was on the top of the tallboy. She could not even turn her head to the side, let alone get up off the bed and go to it. She closed her eyes. Let me sleep, she said to herself, and wake refreshed.

Harry found Cecil Crisp in his office. It resembled a bazaar crammed with swathes of fabric, half-constructed models and merchandize from every department of the store. The place was too small to accommodate its contents. For a moment, Harry stood in the doorway marvelling at how anyone could work amid such apparent chaos. His own office was known for its lack of clutter, the surface of his desk never sullied for long with correspondence or the day's newspapers. Harry liked to deal with everything in a methodical fashion and despatch it, leaving the space around him neat, organized; ordered. The only thing he liked to see on his desk were the fresh flowers that took pride of place. Lately, though, they had induced a sense of sadness and regret, reminding him as they did of Rose.

Cecil Crisp was bent over his drawing board at the far end of the office, his back to Harry. So absorbed was he in what he was doing, he did not notice Harry until he was standing next to him.

Harry clapped him on the shoulder and Cecil straightened up.

'Getting ahead of myself,' he told Harry. 'I had a dream last night about our Christmas windows and decided to sketch out some ideas before I lost them.'

Harry grinned. 'Don't you ever switch off?' he said.

Cecil raised an eyebrow. 'About as often as you do, I'd say.' He gestured at the pencil drawing he was doing. 'Some of Chicago's most recognizable buildings given a holiday feel with coloured lights and so on. Crisp, deep snow. A star-filled sky. Shoppers, full of cheer with bright packages bearing the Marshall Field name.' He beamed at Harry. 'These are only vague ideas right now. The detail will come later.'

Harry never ceased to be amazed by Cecil's dedication to his craft, nor by the quality of his work. Creatively, he was outstanding. Harry knew his head of department had wanted to make a name for himself as a painter, a portrait artist, and had not managed to sell enough of his work to make it viable. There was talk that he had suffered some kind of breakdown. It was Harry's artist friend, Lawrence Porter, who had suggested Cecil Crisp was the man to transform the look of Marshall Field, at the same time advising Harry to go easy on him until he found his feet.

'He needs to get his confidence back,' Lawrence had said.

It had not taken long. What Cecil Crisp had needed was someone to believe in him, allow him the space in which his talent could flourish, and Harry, whose style of managing his staff was always to be generous and fulsome in his praise, proved to be ideal when it came to nurturing the fragile artist.

'It sounds magnificent,' Harry said, already picturing the Christmas windows luring shoppers into the store.

Cecil Crisp looked thoughtful. 'Just wait until the Fair,' he said. 'We will come up with something eye-popping to celebrate.'

A few months before, in the face of strong competition, Chicago had been chosen to host The World's Columbian Exhibition in 1892, which would mark the four hundredth anniversary of Christopher Columbus arriving on America's shores. All the indications were that the fair would prove spectacular, and that nations from all around the world would participate. The civil engineer, George Washington Ferris, was already designing a centrepiece, the likes of which the world had never seen before.

'Have you heard what Ferris is doing?' Cecil Crisp said.

Harry shook his head. 'Only that it will be some kind of colossal structure.'

Cecil peeled back the paper he had been working on to reveal a blank sheet and sketched something on it. 'It will be a wheel, vast in scale,' he said, showing Harry. 'The idea is to attach carriages so that people can ride it and get the best view they'll ever have of the city.' He paused to let this sink in. 'We could use the Ferris idea as the basis for our own display, maybe even construct something to go inside the store, as well as the windows.' He shrugged, tore the paper off the board and screwed it up. 'We'll have to wait and see what Ferris actually comes up with but whatever it is it's going to have the world talking, that's for sure.'

Harry rubbed his chin. 'It's not so far off,' he said, impressed that Cecil was already thinking ahead. 'Less than two years. And you're right about the store reflecting the spirit of the fair, both in our windows and across every department. I know you'll do a great job. That's what I came here to say – the store looks terrific. You worked wonders with the parasols.'

'Ah, the birds in flight,' he said. 'I did take a few liberties to get the effect. Some of the merchandize got – how shall I put it? – remodelled, let's say.'

Harry laughed. 'I take that to mean we won't be able to sell them.'

'They won't be wasted. I can always find a use for things.' He nudged Harry and nodded in the direction of the door. Mary Walters, Harry's secretary, was waiting to speak to him.

'Did I forget an appointment?' he said, going over to her.

'No, Mr Selfridge.' Mary, usually cheerful, was solemn. Harry had a sudden sense of foreboding. 'We've had word to say that Mrs Selfridge is unwell and you're needed urgently at home,' she said.

30.

Rose was not entirely sure what she expected of Clarissa Feldman. Some awkwardness, perhaps. Or an attitude of brazen defiance. And yet when she entered the drawing room, Clarissa greeted her with a smile so warm that Rose felt it could only be genuine. She was thrown. Did Clarissa Feldman feel not the least embarrassment to be carrying on an affair that was being discussed by elements of Chicago society? Clarissa got to her feet and clasped Rose's hand. Again, Rose felt disconcerted. There was no mistaking the spark in Clarissa Feldman's eyes, nor the apparent sincerity in her voice.

'Forgive me Rose for arriving like this with no invitation,' she said. 'I am a very discourteous guest, I know. You have been on my mind, however, and I feel dreadful that we have not yet arranged the luncheon we discussed all those weeks ago at the ball.' She tilted her head on one side. 'I like to think I keep my word and so I have sent a note to Lois and, since I was passing this way anyway, felt I must call and see you in person to apologize.'

Rose felt her insides constrict. 'Why have you any need to apologize?'

'I should have been in touch well before now,' she said. 'I know it's poor of me – will you forgive my lapse?'

Is that all you need forgiveness for? Rose wondered, not sure how to take any of this.

'There's something else too, a more delicate matter, if I may,' she said.

Here it comes, Rose thought, afraid of what Clarissa would say next. She opened her mouth to object, still confused by Clarissa's demeanour. The woman did not seem at all on edge or in any discomfort. Rose was about to say something but Clarissa put up a hand to stop her. She waited until Daphne had poured the coffee and left the room.

'It's to do with Harry,' Clarissa began.

Rose felt a prickle of damp against the back of her neck. No. She did want to hear this. 'Look,' she began.

'Harry is one of our dearest friends. We trust him and know what a thoroughly decent man he is.' Clarissa paused. 'I could give you many instances of his kindness and generosity to the people he loves.'

Rose felt she detected a note of reproach in Clarissa's voice. Feeling under scrutiny she looked away.

Clarissa went on. 'Rose, you may think it is not my business to come here and plead on behalf of Harry. Heaven knows, he would not want it. However, it was clear from the outset how fond he was of you. I don't think I've ever seen him look so happy as the night of the ball. I remember saying as much to Lincoln.' Clarissa waited a moment. The sound of the second hand moving in solid deliberate fashion across the face of the clock on the mantelpiece filled the void.

'I know that he no longer sees you, and that it is not of his choosing,' Clarissa said. 'He does not know why this separation came about.' Rose gazed at her, her mind racing. 'Don't you think it would be right to at least let him know why you turned your back on him?'

Rose almost blurted out what Tyler Collins had told her but something about Clarissa stopped her. She was afraid of saying something that could not be unsaid and would cause irreparable damage. If she hurled an accusation that was founded on the say-so of a jealous suitor how would it look? Now, face to face with Clarissa Feldman, she knew in her heart that Harry was not guilty of having an affair with her. She felt small, foolish.

'Rose?' Clarissa's tone was gentle.

Rose felt her eyes fill with tears. How could she have so readily believed such a dreadful slur? She felt incapable of speech.

Clarissa drank some coffee, allowed a minute or so to pass. 'I know that there are those who feel Harry is not quite good enough, that working his way up from nothing is something to be derided. Well, that's not how Lincoln and I feel about him. We have the utmost respect, not just for what he's achieved but for who he is. I promise, you'll be hard-pressed to find a better man.'

Rose had expected to have the moral high ground with Clarissa Feldman. She had anticipated an unpleasant conversation in which she emerged vindicated while Clarissa was made to slink away, ashamed. Yet Rose was the one feeling shame. She had done something her mother always counselled against and jumped to conclusions she now believed to be wholly false. In taking the word of someone she knew disliked Harry she had judged him when she had no right.

She could not have felt worse.

31.

By the time Harry made it home he was in an agitated state. The note delivered by messenger had told him nothing other than that Lois was unwell and that he should come home as soon as he could manage it. He knew the wording had been carefully chosen in order to minimize his worry. In that, it had failed, since it was inconceivable that Lois would call him back from work unless something was gravely amiss. He could barely contain himself as the carriage made its way from the centre of the city to the suburb of Mount Grace. In his anxious state it seemed the horse was dawdling whereas in fact it was clipping along at some speed. He was jumping out and running in the front door before the driver had even come to a halt.

Harry raced up the stairs to his mother's room. She lay in bed looking years older than when he had left her at the breakfast table only hours earlier. Her skin was waxy, tinged with grey. She managed a smile as he hurried towards her and took her hand. On the far side of the bed Doctor Percy was packing his things into a battered leather bag. He nodded at

Harry, whose eyes darted from his mother to the physician and back.

'Ma, what happened?' he said, kneeling at the side of the bed.

She closed her eyes for a moment, gave his hand a squeeze.

Harry looked to the doctor for an explanation. 'Your mother has suffered an apoplexy, as far as I can tell,' he said. 'She has been fortunate. It was a mild episode.' He snapped shut the bag.

Harry wasn't clear what the term 'apoplexy' meant. Was it some form of heart condition? When he asked Doctor Percy he was told it was to do with an interruption in the blood supply to vital organs. Harry was aghast.

'I'm going to be OK, son,' Lois said, her voice weak.

'Your mother will recover,' Doctor Percy said. 'Treat what happened today as a warning, a sign to take plenty of rest and steer clear of any strain.' He gazed at Lois. 'No overdoing things. And, if you experience any of the symptoms again, call me right away. Any time of the day or night.'

Picking up on the doctor's words, Harry spoke to Lois. 'Have you been feeling unwell?'

She didn't answer.

Doctor Percy frowned. 'I don't think your mother has been in the best of health for several days.'

'I didn't know,' Harry said, shocked.

He felt dreadful. He had been so wrapped up in his own concerns he had failed to notice what was going on right in front of him. He had barely spoken to his mother over breakfast, had not really looked at her. Not closely enough, at any rate. He should have been more vigilant. Guilt washed over him as he thought about the efforts he was making to find his father. Going to Pittsburgh had been of more concern than the wellbeing of his mother. After all she had done for him, he had neglected her just when she needed him. He hung onto her hand, aware of how frail she suddenly appeared. Her eyes were closed and she appeared to be sleeping. He felt he might weep. He might have lost her.

Doctor Percy asked for a word in private and steered Harry out of the room.

'I don't like leaving her,' Harry said, as he accompanied the doctor downstairs.

'I've given her something to make her sleep. It's the best thing for her.'

Harry was pale. 'She looks so ill.'

'She's had a shock but, as I said, what happened was mild. I'd suggest bringing in nursing staff to be with her for the next week or so, just as a precaution – if you're agreeable.'

Harry nodded. Whatever his mother needed. 'I can put things on hold, be with her as much as she needs me.' He would get Mary to cancel all his meetings. It went through his mind he was supposed to meet with Marshall Field that afternoon. The partnership was up for discussion. No matter. That would have to be shelved for now. Whatever was in his diary, the whole caboodle could wait. He felt an ache inside his chest at the thought he had been putting business matters and his own ambitions ahead of Lois. At the same time he knew that much of his drive to succeed stemmed from a desire to make her proud and provide for her the best possible lifestyle.

He thought back to two nights ago when she had changed her mind about going to the theatre with him, making an excuse at the last minute about being tired. Was that all that it had been? No. He now knew she was feeling unwell and doing her utmost to conceal it from him. His mother was the most selfless, uncomplaining woman there was. Again, he felt an urge to shed tears. All that he was and had done with his life thus far was thanks to Lois, yet when she was ill and needed him he had not even been aware that something was amiss. In his anguish it came to him how much he missed Rose. How he wished she was there.

'I'll make arrangements for a nurse to come, if you're happy,' Doctor Percy said, breaking in on his thoughts.

Harry said that was fine with him. He had no intention of going back to the store until Lois showed signs of improvement. In the meantime, he would stay with her around the clock. He thought about the armchair in her room. He would be comfortable enough spending the night in it.

It was as if the doctor knew what he was thinking. 'Can I offer some advice?'

'Of course.'

Doctor Percy frowned. 'It won't do your mother any good if you get overtired and put yourself under excessive strain. What I would suggest is that, yes, cut back on your workload a little, spend some extra time here if you can – *but* once the nurse is here, let her do her job.'

'Is there anything I can do, meanwhile?'

'She'll sleep for the next several hours now. I'll see if I can get some help here this evening, then you need to rest.' He took in Harry's chalky pallor. 'Believe me, you need to look after yourself. You've had an almighty shock.'

'Do you know what caused this?'

'I can't say for sure. It's not uncommon with advancing years.'

Advancing years. Harry hated to think his mother was growing old.

'I'll look in on her in the morning, see how she's doing,' Doctor Percy said. 'Remember what I told you.'

Once the doctor had gone, Harry went back upstairs and pulled the armchair close to Lois's bed. She was sleeping, at peace, it seemed. The lines on her face seemed deeper, more pronounced. He reached out and stroked her hair.

Tears ran down his cheeks and onto the pillow.

32.

For three days Harry stayed at home. Despite what he had been told about making sure to get sufficient rest he kept up a bedside vigil, hunched in the armchair close to Lois, allowing himself little sleep. He did all he could to stay awake, even when overcome with exhaustion, feeling that to succumb to sleep would be to abandon Lois, despite the presence of the nurse. Throughout the night a lamp remained lit and in its soft glow Harry could see his mother in repose. She lay utterly still, occasionally opening her eyes for a few precious moments. When he saw she was awake he would scramble from the chair and take her hand, murmur a few reassuring words. It was as much as Lois could do to smile before her eyes closed and she drifted back into a deep sleep. Harry was concerned she was sleeping too much but the doctor was adamant it was a vital element of her recovery. Each day he administered strong sedation to ensure Lois got complete rest. While it was not Harry's style to relinquish control, in this instance he had no choice but to accept what the doctor told him.

During the long hours of darkness, odd fragments of memories crowded into Harry's mind. He had an image of his childhood home in Ripon, of coming in to find his mother making bread. Her face had lit up at the sight of him but there was something in her eyes that even as a child troubled him. Sadness. Weariness. He was not sure. As a small boy of perhaps six or seven years old he had known enough to appreciate life was not easy, despite his mother's relentlessly cheerful outlook. Now he appreciated just how important her upbeat attitude had been to their survival. She could have been broken by poverty, by the loss of her husband, the deaths of two of her boys. Instead, she had gathered up every shred of inner strength and kept going, without complaint; without self-pity. It was her example that had made Harry who he was.

Harry did all he could to stay awake through the night but still fell in and out of a state that was something between sleep and wakefulness. Even when he slept, he felt he was awake. His mind never quite gave him peace. Thoughts flooded in, some conscious, some dreams, concerning his search for his father. At one point he saw Lois coming down the stairs in her nightgown, ghostly and pale, tears streaming down her face. He cried out and woke with a start to find her sleeping peacefully. On the far side of the bed, the nurse gave him a curious look. Three nights without any real sleep were taking their toll.

Harry was off his food. He had no appetite. Throughout the day, he consumed little more than coffee. Each morning, Doctor Percy arrived to check on his patient and while Lois was doing well and getting the prescribed amount of sleep,

Harry was beginning to look exhausted. Shadows had appeared under his eyes. The doctor took a dim view. Since there was a nurse on hand during the day and another to cover nights it made no sense for Harry to wear himself out.

'You need to listen to what I'm saying,' Doctor Percy told him. 'Your mother is doing fine. She will make a good recovery, but I really wouldn't want to be in your shoes when she finds out you've been putting your own health at risk for no good reason.' He waited a moment before adding, 'And, count on it, I *will* be putting her in the picture.'

'I'm fine, doc,' Harry said.

'You look like hell, if you don't mind my being blunt. You need sleep. If you carry on like this you'll be no use to your mother.' To Harry's surprise he took him by the elbow and propelled him to a full-length mirror. 'Take a look.'

Harry winced. He looked hollow-eyed and dishevelled. Like a man deprived of sleep for three days, in fact. Beside him, the doctor, in his immaculate suit, crisp white shirt and grey tie, was a model of good grooming.

'Go and bathe and freshen up,' Doctor Percy instructed. 'I don't suppose you've eaten this morning.' The look on Harry's face told him he was correct in his assumption. 'I'll ask for breakfast to be prepared for you in, say, thirty minutes or so?'

Harry put on the red silk tie his mother liked. When she was well enough to properly take in her surroundings again the last thing he wanted was her to find him looking as if he was the one in need of medical attention. The doctor was right. Lois depended on him, in which case he had a duty to keep himself in good shape.

Downstairs, he ate a breakfast of ham and eggs and went easy on the coffee. He had felt his nerves jangling during the last few days, no doubt thanks to all the coffee he was getting through on top of the anxiety he was feeling. Just as he was finishing breakfast, he heard the doorbell go. As word had spread about Lois notes and gifts had been arriving from friends. Some had wanted to visit but he had said it was too soon. The first to be in touch was Marshall Field, within hours of Harry hurrying home from the store. He had sent flowers for Lois and told Harry to take as long as he needed.

The door to the breakfast room opened and the Selfridge's butler came in.

'Sorry to disturb you sir, but there's a visitor,' Ralph said.

Harry wasn't in the mood to see anyone. 'Can't you put them off?'

Ralph retreated into the hall. A moment later he was back. 'I do apologize, Mr Selfridge, but they seem rather reluctant to leave,' he said.

Harry felt a prickle of annoyance. Who would be thick-skinned enough to call at a time like this? Surely everyone in Chicago knew that Lois was ill and that peace and quiet were the order of the day. He was really not in the mood to entertain, whoever it was. He sighed. 'I can't imagine what can be so important that it can't wait.'

'I'm afraid the lady wouldn't say but she was rather insistent.'

The lady. It suddenly came to him he had been due to meet Clarissa Feldman for lunch the day before. Since it was a private engagement it had not been in his diary at the office and therefore his secretary would not have been in touch to cancel. Still, a note had come from Clarissa the day after Lois became unwell expressing her concern. She, of all people, would understand. Perhaps she had come to offer assistance.

Harry went into the hall. In a shadowy recess, on the velvet chaise longue, beneath a painting that had been a gift from Lawrence Porter, his visitor waited. Harry caught his breath.

Rose.

33.

For a moment neither of them said anything. Harry was dumbfounded. Rose coming to see him at home was the last thing he would have have expected. He faced her across the hallway, finding he was unable to cover the distance that separated them. It was as if he could not persuade his legs to move. Out of nowhere, the tiredness he had been battling for days threatened again to consume him and he had an urge to sink to the floor and close his eyes. He blinked several times in quick succession, not taking his eyes off her, the look on his face giving away the sheer incomprehension he felt at finding her there.

Rose got up. She too seemed unable to cross to where he stood. An expanse of black and white tiles lay between them; a checkers board. Neither one of them sure whose move it was.

Eventually, Harry spoke her name. His voice was soft, uncertain. It gave away his sense of bewilderment and something else; the hurt he felt at what had happened between them. The spell was broken and Rose moved quickly to stand in front of him. She took his hands in hers and held them for a moment. Harry was unsure and gazed into her eyes, registering what seemed to him to be concern and sadness. For what, though? The collapse of their relationship, or the state of Lois's health? The sight of Rose hit him hard, unexpectedly so. After days of worry and lack of sleep he had a sense of being in poor control of his emotions. Everything seemed heightened, jittery. For one brief moment he wondered if he was imagining her there in front of him.

'Is there somewhere we can sit for a moment?' Rose said, letting go of his hands.

Harry struggled to pull himself together. Without her holding onto him he felt he might lose his balance. The doctor had been right about getting some sleep. He was feeling the effects of not having enough now, all right. He nodded and led her into the room where he had been having breakfast.

'I'm sorry, did I interrupt you eating?' Rose said, seeing the things set out on the table.

'I was just finishing,' Harry said, surprised at how chilly he sounded all of a sudden.

Rose seemed flustered and hung back in the doorway. 'It was wrong of me to come like this,' she said. 'I should leave.'

He was tempted to let her go. She had pushed him away for no reason he understood without even the courtesy of an explanation. It went through his mind to show Rose the door without hearing whatever it was she had come to say. Thinking about Lois upstairs, he changed his mind. Life is short, he told himself. Everything can change in a moment, in less than a fraction of a second. You may never get another chance. He gestured at the settee at the far end of the room.

'You're here now,' he said, not able to keep the hurt he felt out of his voice. 'Let me organize some coffee and we'll talk.'

Rose remained in the doorway.

'Assuming you *want* to talk,' Harry said. 'I'm guessing there's something you came here to say.'

After a moment's hesitation she came into the room and sat on the edge of the sofa, straight-backed, uncomfortable. She too looked pale, Harry thought, and a little more slender than he had remembered. It went through his mind that something bad may also have been going on in her life and he felt a pang of guilt. Had Rose really been unwell? While he was baffled by her treatment of him he reminded himself that he had yet to hear what she had to say. There may, after all, be an explanation, he told himself. Certainly, it had taken courage for her to come to see him, at the risk of being turned away. The least he could do now was not leap to any conclusions. Going back a few weeks when his heart was breaking, Lois had told him he should ask Rose what had led to her sudden decision to back away from him. Well, now he had the chance. That was what he would do. Rose took off her gloves and placed them on the table at the side of the settee. Harry excused himself and went to arrange for fresh coffee to be brought in.

Rose looked around the room. It was the first time she had been to the house. She was not sure what she had imagined but the furnishings and artwork were impressive. She had recognized the painting in the entrance hall as one of Lawrence Porter's. It was unusual in that it was done in deep dark blues and what Rose would describe as a blackish magenta. It was brooding, original. She closed her eyes, remembering the night at the Monet exhibition, the laughter before Tyler blundered in threatening to ruin everything, not managing to. Harry had shown dignity that night. She recalled meeting Lawrence Porter and the high regard he had for Harry. They had not had their promised dinner, the three of them, after all. And whose fault was that? She was the one who had pulled up short on a relationship that had made her happier than she had ever been. You fool, Rose, she told herself, feeling her eyes fill with tears. She blinked them away, telling herself Harry had enough to contend with already. Having turned up without notice, to break down while his mother lay ill upstairs would be the height of selfishness. She took a handkerchief from her purse and dabbed at her eyes.

She had thought about what she wanted to say, gone over it in her mind a number of times. She had even written it down, pages and pages covered in crossings-out and corrections. By the time she had finished she could not even read her own writing and had torn the pages to tiny pieces and thrown them away. She wished she had been able to see Harry at the store. Feeling not in the least bit brave, she had hoped it might be easier to sit down with him in the restaurant at Marshall Field. A public place, she surmised, would be safer. For the second time in the space of a few weeks, she had gone, chosen the table she had sat at with Harry the first time they spoke, and waited, certain he would appear. Two hours had passed during which she felt increasingly embarrassed, as if it was clear to every other person there, waiters included, that she was engaged in some sort of undignified pursuit of Harry Selfridge.

She finally forced herself to ask if Mr Selfridge was expected. He was not in the store, she was told. No, no one knew when he would be back. He was tending to a family emergency. Rose could find out nothing more. She had been shocked, certain that the emergency must involve Lois and that it had to be serious for Harry to be at home. She knew how much Lois meant to him, and vice versa. They only had each other. If something had happened, he would be frantic with worry. For the rest of the day she had agonized over what to do, finally deciding to go and see him, knowing there was every chance he would not admit her. She would not blame him. He might just see her, though. She could, at least, give it a go. The guilt she felt at having pushed him away became almost unbearable. Had she not been so unfair in dropping him at the first hint of gossip she could have been there for him, and for Lois, at their time of need. She had let him down, badly.

She felt like weeping.

When Harry came back into the room he saw at once that Rose was on the verge of tears and gabbled something about the coffee being on its way, how he was drinking way too much of it at the moment, practically operating solely on endless cups, doing all he could to keep up the chatter in order to give her time to regain her composure. It was as much to spare his own feelings as hers. He was already wrung out over Lois. Whatever Rose wanted with him, he was in no condition to cope with any kind of emotional outpouring.

They sat without saying anything, Harry at the opposite end of the settee from Rose, watching her closely. To his relief, she seemed to have recovered. *No tears, please*, he thought. Ralph brought in a tray of coffee and left it with them.

'Can I pour some?' Harry said, breaking the silence.

'Thank you.'

He poured coffee into a delicate white china cup and set it on the table next to the gloves Rose had placed there. They were red, he noticed, almost the same shade as the tie he was wearing.

He sat back down. Rose gave him a small smile.

In a rush, the feelings he had been forced to bury without knowing why flooded back and with them came a painful sense of injustice. Coming here like this was wrong of her. She was toying with him. Anger flared inside.

'What is it you want from me, Rose?' he said, the chill back in his voice.

34.

A week to the day following Lois's collapse Harry was back at the store. When the doctor called, the day after Rose had visited, he declared Lois well enough to get up. She was helped from the bed and into the chair Harry had been occupying night after night, and the curtains were drawn back to allow sun to stream into the room. Having had the appearance of a sick bay for several days, her bedroom now resumed its usual character. It was remarkable how well Lois looked. At lunchtime, food was sent up on a tray and she managed some of the broth the cook had made especially for her, as well as a few mouthfuls of rice pudding. In the space of a few hours she was beginning to look more like her old self again. Harry remained vigilant, searching for any signs that they were pushing her too hard, too fast. Lois seemed in good spirits, however, which was heartening to see. Only a few days before he had feared he would lose her. Now, the colour was returning to her cheeks and while she still looked tired Harry had faith she would be fully restored in time. According to the doctor, she was on course to make a complete recovery. In the meantime, the nurses would remain and Doctor Percy would reduce his house calls to every other day.

On the morning he returned to work, Harry felt anxious at the prospect of leaving Lois, although he knew she was in good hands. Halfway into town, he had almost got the carriage driver to turn around and take him home again. All that stopped him was picturing the look on his mother's face when he admitted he was checking up on her. Seeing Lois so ill had made him fearful and forced him to re-think his approach to life based on this renewed understanding that nothing could be taken for granted. *Life is short* had become his new mantra. Harry was thinking hard about what really mattered, getting his priorities straight. Lois came first, no question about it. He vowed to be much sharper where she was concerned. If he hadn't taken his eye off the ball he would have known she was sick ahead of her collapse. He might have been able to prevent the apoplexy if only he had been paying proper attention. It made him want to kick himself that what had distracted him from his mother's wellbeing was thinking about his missing father. There was an irony there. He still had to decide what to do about Pittsburgh. When it came to working out his next move he found his new life-is-short philosophy (which wasn't so different from his old seize-the-moment attitude) was not much help. On the one hand, there was no time to lose. If his father was still alive he was getting on. What was it the doctor had said of Lois? Advancing years. Well, that also applied to Robert Selfridge, assuming he was still alive. If he had survived the Civil War he might be nursing an injury or some kind of mental incapacity. Harry needed to make haste if he was truly serious about finding him. Then again, seeing Lois taken ill had made him reluctant to make another trip just yet. Going to Pittsburgh would mean another overnight stay. More, perhaps, if he managed to find his father. The thought stopped him in his tracks. He knew he had not allowed himself to fully consider what the repercussions of such an outcome would be. What would it do to Lois? It was not something he wanted to address. For once, it was far from clear-cut to him what the best course of action might be.

On his first day back Harry resumed his usual routine of walking the shop floor, making time to speak to staff. He was touched by how happy they all seemed to be to see him. In the loading bay, he sought out Danny Donovan and asked how the wedding plans were going. They had set a date, Danny said; November 11. 'We wanted it to be this year and both of us liked the sound of eleven-eleven,' he said, pleased with himself.

Harry agreed that eleven-eleven, as Danny put it, sounded very good, indeed.

'How is Mrs Selfridge, sir?' he asked.

'She's doing well, thank you,' Harry said. 'On the mend.'

As Harry made his way to his office he felt elated, full of energy. It had been the right decision to return to work, exactly what he needed. Finally, he would sit down with Marshall Field and have the discussion that was supposed to have taken place the week before. The question of the partnership needed to be resolved. It was up there on Harry's list of top priorities. He could not afford to let his career bump along if he was to achieve his ambition of one day owning his own store. He had to drive things forward, generate more income, enough to give him serious purchasing power in the future. He felt confident he could make Marshall see his point of view.

As he strolled along the corridor to his office, Mary, his secretary was waiting.

'Good to have you back, Mr Selfridge,' she said, beaming.

'Very good to be here,' he said.

'We're all so pleased that Mrs Selfridge is doing well.'

'It's been quite a week but she is doing just great. She's a real inspiration.' He checked his pocket watch. 'Mr Oliver is due in a few minutes?'

'I'm here, Harry,' came a voice from the far end of the corridor. Drew Oliver strode towards him. 'I even brought you a newspaper.' He handed over a copy of the *Herald*. 'Nothing much worth reading, I'm afraid. It's been dull copy without you here to pep things up.'

Harry laughed. 'Come on in, Drew. You can bring me up to date on all I've missed this past week.'

'As I say, all rather uneventful.' He winked at Mary. 'You've no idea how much I've missed you, Harry. It's hard going, scraping about for stories with you out of commission.'

In the privacy of Harry's office, Drew Oliver delivered what little news he had from Pittsburgh regarding Harry's father.

'Thompson spoke to some of the neighbours. Apparently, the woman we spoke to on Charlotte doesn't live alone.' He paused. 'One said there definitely was a man living there.' Harry frowned. 'Was?'

'Still is, perhaps. Keeps himself to himself, doesn't get out much.' Another pause. 'Rumour has it he was injured in the Civil War.'

Harry sat in silence, taking this in. Had his father actually been there when they paid that visit a few weeks back? The movement he had detected in the hallway came back to him. The thought that his father might have been a few yards away, hiding in the gloomy little property, made him feel depressed. Again, he wondered at the merit of hunting him down. If he was alive, perhaps he did not want to be found.

'We should get back down there,' Drew was saying. 'I can't help feeling we're close.'

Harry thought about it. From out of nowhere a feeling came crashing in, warning him that the search for his father would not have a happy ending. He felt a cold shiver along the back of his neck. He was chasing shadows, putting energy into something filled with uncertainty when what had happened in the last week had told him to focus on what he knew; the here and now. His father was a ghost. Lois was real. Did it really make sense to take off for Pittsburgh – being less than candid with his mother about why he was going – on what could turn out to be little more than a wild goose chase?

'I need time to take all this in,' Harry said.

'Of course. Just don't leave it too long. You never know what's round the corner.'

'That's what last week taught me. Trouble is, I don't know if the lesson I was meant to take from it was about concentrating on what really matters, the here and now-' he hesitated and let out a sigh. 'Instead of chasing crazy dreams.'

Drew was watching him closely. 'I hope I never live to see the day when Harry Selfridge gives up on chasing crazy dreams.'

35.

Rose could not stop thinking about Harry. The day she had arrived at his home she was sure of what she wanted to say and determined for him to hear her out. What happened afterwards was up to him. Their meeting had not gone anything like according to plan. She had not anticipated how she would feel on coming face to face with him. The moment she had stood in front of him in the hall she had feared her heart would stop beating. It was as if a vice had closed around it and was squeezing hard. She could not get her breath, let alone find her voice and had stood there mute. He looked tired, worn down with the worry. Later, searching for a word to accurately describe his demeanour, she had come up with *pained*. That was it. Not only was he desperately worried about his sick mother, in his eyes there was hurt. Rose understood that even if she was not the cause she was certainly a major contributor. The sight of Harry looking so wretched had made her mouth dry and robbed her of the capacity to say all that she had intended to. It had been quite a speech she had prepared. She had wanted to make him understand that she had been duped into thinking ill of him. In truth, she had hoped she would not have to admit that the responsibility for the breakdown in their relationship lay with her. Yet hadn't she chosen to listen to the poisonous words uttered by Tyler Collins? It had been in her power to disregard him and yet she did not. No fancy speech was necessary. All she had really needed to say was a heartfelt *sorry*. In the end, she had struggled to say very much at all. Having enquired after Lois she found her courage deserting her. *Coward*, she thought, as she dodged the matter she was there to address and instead asked if Harry needed extra help while Lois was ill. He had seemed nonplussed that she should even be offering, and no wonder. Rose hardly counted as a close and valued friend, the sort you would entrust with the care of your sick mother. Not now.

Not after the way she had behaved.

She had sat on the settee sipping coffee, her throat so tight she could barely get the scorching liquid down, all the while wishing she had not come. It had been a mistake. Her very presence seemed to have had a detrimental effect on Harry. His weariness seemed to intensify. Although he was within touching distance it was as if an unseen obstacle lay between them preventing her from getting any closer. He was beyond reach. She detected something almost hazardous about him and imagined that were she to put a hand on his arm she would be met with a powerful electrical shock. Harry had been distant, distracted, suffering. Her being there only made things worse. She had made a poor attempt at putting things right. Knowing she had failed filled her with despair.

Harry returned home from the store to be met with the sound of the piano. In the drawing room, Lois was playing something haunting, vaguely familiar. She seemed so absorbed in the music she did not hear him come in. In profile, his mother looked serene, content, her hands picking out the notes with assurance. Sensing his presence, she turned and smiled.

'I didn't mean to stop you,' Harry said.

'I was about to call it a day anyway,' Lois said. 'I'm out of practise, I'm afraid.'

'What was it you were playing?'

She laughed. 'I couldn't tell you. Remember McCormick Hall last year? Something we heard played there has been on my mind, going round and round. I don't even remember who the composer was but I wanted to try and play it. *My* version, anyway. Really, all I'm doing is a rough approximation based on what is probably a very poor memory.'

Lois had an excellent ear for music. It astonished Harry that she could play piano at all, having had no formal lessons, and somehow recreate with a degree of accuracy music she had heard played in various concert halls.

'It sounded to me you were doing a pretty good job,' he said. 'As long as you're not overdoing things. You're only just getting back on your feet.'

Lois closed the piano lid and stood up. 'I've been back on my feet for a couple of days now, son,' she said. 'I can't sit around here doing nothing for hours at a stretch – not unless you want me to die of boredom.'

She was looking so much brighter, the sparkle back in her eyes. Harry could barely comprehend how fast she had faded nor the speed with which she seemed to be bouncing back to robust good health. He remained wary, unwilling to take it for granted that the crisis was truly past. At the same time, he had no wish to see his energetic mother become an invalid. Every bit of progress she made was to be encouraged.

'I'm arranging tickets for the Chicago Symphony Orchestra at the Auditorium in October,' he said.

Lois beamed. 'That's just the tonic I need,' she said.

Over dinner, Lois brought up the delicate subject of Rose.

'I received a kind note from her,' she said, watching Harry closely. 'I wish you'd tell me what's going on between the two of you.'

Harry rested his cutlery on the side of his plate. On the advice of Doctor Percy, the food they were eating was much lighter now. Fish, vegetables, lean cuts of meat. No rich sauces. Harry had been surprised at how good it tasted.

'I don't know what to tell you,' he said. 'Rose came to see me when you were sick.'

Lois frowned. 'She was here?'

'I can't tell you how taken aback I was to find her out in the hallway.' He shook his head, remembering. 'She took my breath away.'

Lois saw the hurt in his eyes and remained silent.

'I thought she had come to tell me what went wrong, why she changed her mind-' another shake of the head '-about us. In the end, other than to ask about you she said very little. Not a word about cutting me dead since the Fourth of July ball.'

Lois was thoughtful. 'Maybe you took her breath away too,' she said. Harry gave her a questioning look. 'When it came to it perhaps she wasn't able to say whatever was on her mind. It can't have been easy coming here in the first place and then, well, who knows? You won't have been at your best. It may be she felt it was the wrong moment. Timing can be everything, you know.'

Harry thought back to the morning Rose had visited, shortly after he had faced his reflection in the mirror and found himself to be drawn and hollow-eyed. His appearance might well have thrown her. He was conscious too that he had closed down in her presence and kept her at arms-length. At that point, he had not felt able to take on anything else that might prove emotionally trying, not with Lois so ill. He wondered if Lois was right and that Rose had not been able to speak as she had intended.

'I don't suppose you were able to say very much either,' Lois said. 'I know how much you wanted answers, probably still do, and you know my feelings – it doesn't help anyone to carry around a weight of unresolved hurt. You're in pain and so is she, I'd say.'

'It's not my doing,' Harry said, with some vehemence.

'No. You've been treated badly by someone you cared deeply about.' Lois waited a moment. She felt sure Harry still cared for Rose. 'Don't you want to find out why?'

36.

He had to be crazy. It was asking for trouble. *More* trouble, he reminded himself. And yet, once the idea had taken hold he had been unable to shake it. It was like one of those orchestral pieces that got inside Lois's head and wouldn't let go until she sat down at the piano and played it out as best she could. Well, now he was about to see how things played out, except at stake was more than the odd bad note.

He had given careful consideration to what Lois had said about Rose coming to see him, the timing of her visit, and the awkward atmosphere that had prevailed. When it came to the wedge already in place between the two of them Harry had only made things worse, determined she would not feel able to speak freely. He knew exactly what he had done that day and why. He had wanted Rose to suffer as he had. Lois had been right when she said it was the wrong moment. In fact, it was, quite possibly, the worst moment.

He was not one for having regrets. Once something began to prey on his mind his habit was to deal with it. Well, he would deal with his feelings for Rose once and for all.

He had arranged a carriage to bring her to the restaurant at the Wellington Hotel on the corner of South Wabash Avenue. Harry got there early and waited at a table at the back of the restaurant. He felt calm, composed. It made sense to talk things through and move on. That was all he wanted.

While he waited he took in his surroundings. He rarely ate at the Wellington but the restaurant was well thought out with the right amount of space between the tables so that diners had some privacy. He liked it that the windows had pebbled glass so that the outside world felt at bay. On the street it was busy, the usual city bustle, yet inside was a haven of peace. It was clever how they had managed that. They don't have flowers on the tables, though, he thought, pleased he had come up with at least one special touch at Marshall Field.

The Wellington was clearly popular. It had filled up since he arrived and he raised a hand in greeting to the people he recognized, mainly business associates. He really had to do something about the restaurant at Marshall Field. Clearly, the business was there to be had and it made sense to create a much more spacious restaurant in the store.

He looked up to see Rose coming towards him. She was dressed in a shade of blue against which the whiteness of her skin was startling. Again, he had the feeling that she was more slender than she had been. He felt his heart contract and fought to get his feelings under control. He had made up his mind to treat the lunch like a business meeting, a fact-finding exercise, and that was what he would do. Afterwards, he would close the file on the whole sorry mess and let it go.

Harry got up to greet her. The uncertainty in her eyes pulled at him and at once he had the feeling the cool-headed approach he had been so determined to take was in danger of collapsing. 'Thanks for agreeing to meet me,' he said, working at keeping a note of formality in his voice, not quite managing it.

Rose held his gaze as she sat down.

Harry asked if she would like something to drink and she asked for water, which was already on the table. The waiter poured her a glass and retreated.

Rose removed her gloves, the same pair she had been wearing when she had come to the house to see Harry. She picked up the menu that had been placed in front of her and put it aside.

'Harry, there's something I need to say.' Her voice sounded strained, as if it might break. 'I owe you an apology – an almighty one.' She took a breath. 'I treated you very badly.'

Before Harry was able to reply she went on. 'There's nothing I can say to excuse my behaviour, I know that, and I don't expect you will. I accept that. You were only ever good to me and I want you to know how truly sorry I am and how much I regret-' she came to a halt, took another breath –'how very much I regret ruining what was a special relationship.'

Harry was lost for words. Regret. Was she hoping to turn back the clock and pick things up with him again? He had no idea what to say.

The waiter appeared to take their order and Harry let him know they had yet to decide. Whether either of them would feel like eating now he had no idea. His mind shot forward to picking his way through a plate of food, each mouthful a struggle. He gave Rose a pleading look and saw in her eyes a reflection of his own feelings of sorrow and discomfort.

'Say something,' she said, attempting a smile that didn't quite come off.

He gazed at her, unable to speak. His head was swimming. What he felt about her was still there, not far from the surface, he knew that. Yet by her own admission she had treated him badly. He gulped down the water from the crystal tumbler in front of him. Almost as soon as he put the glass back down the waiter was there filling it up. Harry nodded his thanks. 'Give us a few minutes,' he told the waiter. 'No interruptions. I'll let you know when we're ready to order.' If we actually get round to having any food, Harry thought.

His collar felt tight, a sure sign of anxiety. Inside, he was churned up. Any appetite he might have had was gone. He had no idea how he was going to get through lunch. To imagine he could be with Rose like this and behave as if she were a business colleague had been foolish. He should have known the mere sight of her would be enough to derail him.

'I'm truly sorry, Harry,' she said again.

He stared at the table, at the embossed snowy cloth. Irish linen, he thought. A nice touch. Matching napkins in ornate silver rings. Weighty silver cutlery. He pictured someone in a room off the kitchen polishing it all for hours on end to make sure it gleamed before it got anywhere near the restaurant. Irish linen. When he expanded the Marshall Field restaurant that was what would be on the tables. He glanced at Rose. The look she gave him was enough to shatter his heart. She appeared ashen, as if the words she had uttered so far had cost her dearly. He felt an urge to reach for her hand and tell her he understood. Not that he could. He did not understand any of it. Nothing made sense. *You were only ever good to me.* She was the one who had behaved badly, that much he understood.

But why?

37.

Harry was walking the floor of the fashion department when he spotted a familiar figure browsing, examining bolts of flame orange and red silk that had been unfurled, hung with tassels and feathers, and arranged to suggest what lay behind them was an exotic club. The work of Cecil Crisp, no mistake. Harry ducked out of sight behind a mannequin, to the surprise of one of the junior assistants, Polly Grace. She gave him a curious look and Harry mouthed at her not to give him away. Polly retreated behind a counter and made minor unnecessary adjustments to a display of lace edging, all the while keeping an eye on Harry. He smiled to himself. The staff already had him down as a maverick. It wouldn't hurt to be considered on the eccentric side too. He sneaked a look from behind his hiding place to ensure his quarry was looking the other way then, in a few stealthy strides, was upon her. He winked at Polly Grace before booming, 'Good day.'

The unwary customer jumped with fright.

Clarissa Feldman spun around. 'Harry! You frightened me half to death creeping up like that.'

Harry caught sight of Polly in the background, the lace edging she had been fussing over forgotten, grinning in delight.

'I'm sorry, Clarissa, you were so caught up in eyeing up that fabric I couldn't resist. You looked to be miles away.'

Clarissa narrowed her eyes. 'I was imagining myself celebrating Christmas in a gown made of this rather fine silk. The red, I was thinking. That was until you almost made my heart stop.'

'Let me make it up to you. Join me in my office for tea?'

'I might need something a little stronger. My nerves are shot to bits.'

Harry had not seen Clarissa since before Lois took ill and had yet to reschedule lunch.

'I owe you an apology,' he said, when they were settled in his office. 'I don't think I even let you know I couldn't make lunch a few weeks ago. It went right out of my mind.'

She waved away his concerns. 'You don't need to say a word about it.'

'It's been on my mind to see you but time seems to be running away with me.'

'I've been wanting to see you too,' she said. Harry waited for her to explain. 'I went to see a friend of yours. Rose Buckingham.'

He felt a jolt of anxiety. 'I didn't know the two of you were close.'

'No, but the two of you were at one time. More than close. I thought you were settling down and then …' she gave a shrug. 'I don't know what happened and it's none of my business but you're my friend, Harry, and I care about you. I know you've been hurting so I let Rose know she had let the best man in Chicago slip through her hands. Foolish woman.'

'When was this?'

'Ages ago. Before anyone knew Lois was unwell. Look, I know what you're going to say and you're right. I shouldn't interfere.' She leaned across and squeezed his hand. 'I just couldn't bear seeing you so unhappy, not when you'd been walking on air at the ball. It was obvious how much you cared for her and, in all honesty, I'd have said the feeling was mutual. She was radiant that night. So-' she sighed- 'I had a few words.' Harry gave her a look. 'Nothing terrible, so don't worry.'

Harry was silent for a moment.

'Please don't be cross, Harry. It's what friends are for.'

'It's not that. I appreciate you sticking your neck out for me.'

He told Clarissa about Rose coming to see him and their lunch at the Wellington when she had apologized and owned up about what was behind her abrupt decision to stop seeing him. The discovery that Tyler Collins had blackened both Harry's name and that of his good friend, Clarissa, had made him furious. He had wanted to find him and knock his block off. According to Rose, however, Collins had already left town. Harry could barely countenance that Rose had so readily swallowed gossip fed from such a dubious source. Tyler Collins of all people. Harry was not sure he would ever be able to forgive her.

He told Clarissa the story, all of it, while she listened, not interrupting. When he had finished he sat back in his chair. For a moment Clarissa said nothing and then to his surprise burst out laughing.

'What's funny?' Harry said.

'Is that *all* that sent things off track with Rose?'

'*All*? Isn't it enough?'

'From what you're saying, nothing actually went wrong between the two of you. You didn't argue or fall out or get bored.' Harry wasn't sure where this was going. 'What happened was you came under attack from a malicious third party, someone who couldn't stand to see the two of you happy.'

'Rose didn't have to believe him. It's not like he twisted her arm.'

'No, but I bet he was convincing enough and, from what you've said, it's not just you who suffered. OK, you came off worse, but the two of you have been in purgatory from what I can see.' Harry seemed about to object but Clarissa hadn't finished. 'If you still care for each other – and it's obvious you do – you can put things right.'

Harry wasn't sure about that.

'Pick up the pieces. Move on.' Clarissa's tone softened. 'Look at what you've just been through with Lois. We never know what's coming our way, when something will come along and rob us of our happiness. My feeling is that life is way too precious, way too short, to pass up on the good things. Rose is one of those good things, Harry. At least she might be. You were just getting to know one another when that idiot

Collins wrecked things. Don't let him win. Learn from it. From now on, if something happens, *talk* to each other.'

'What bothers me is that she was so ready to think the worst of me.'

'She was falling for you, Harry, and that made her vulnerable. She was probably wondering if she could trust her feelings, if she was getting carried away, if it was all too good to be true ... then someone she thought she knew well – a *respected architect*, no less – made her believe she had got it all horribly wrong.' Clarissa gave him a sharp look. 'Give her a chance. She made an almighty blunder but don't tell me you've never leapt to the wrong conclusion about anyone?'

Harry was about to insist that he most certainly had not when he remembered suspecting Rose of concealing a prior involvement with Tyler Collins. In his hurt, Harry had come to believe the only reason she had shown any interest in him in the first place was to make Collins jealous. He had been convinced she had used him, something he now knew to be way off the mark. He was only glad he had not given voice to his suspicions. He shot Clarissa a sheepish look. She need never know.

'When I met Lincoln one of his best friends tried to destroy our relationship,' Clarissa said. Harry looked at her in astonishment. 'It was someone Lincoln had known all his life. A trusted, supposedly loyal friend who could not stand me. He thought I was after Lincoln's money, that a woman so much younger could not possibly love him. I was so hurt I almost walked away.' She gave him a defiant look. 'I didn't, though, because I knew my feelings were real and I wasn't about to let someone wreck what might have been the only chance I was ever going to get to find happiness. Love is rare, Harry, and contrary to what some people might tell you it's in short supply. Plenty people go through life without ever finding it.' She took his hand again. 'Don't let that be you.'

After a moment, Harry said, 'Does Lincoln know you think I'm the best man in Chicago?'

38.

Rose had spent the morning in the summer house at the end of the garden. She told her mother she was painting and asked to be left alone but in fact she had barely picked up a brush. Her subject was a still life, an arrangement of the dried flowers from those sent by Harry. She had begun well enough but could not concentrate. She sat on a bench in the shade deep in thought, her mind harking back to the day she had met Harry for lunch at the Wellington. She could not forget the look on his face when she told him the reason for her sudden disappearance from his life. His feelings were all too plain to see. He had appeared utterly devastated but had said almost nothing. She guessed the shock was too great for him to comprehend. She bent her head and covered her face with her hands. How could she have been so stupid?

When she heard someone say her name and looked up she found Harry standing a few feet away. 'Your mother said you were painting.' He glanced at the canvas, at the dried flowers on the stand in front of it. 'Am I disturbing you?'

Rose felt her throat go dry. Her dress was an old one dotted with oil paint, her hair all over the place. Whenever she painted she tended to pull strands loose from their grips until she had a mass of wild-looking tendrils. She guessed she looked an utter mess while Harry was immaculately turned out. Her cheeks reddened. In her wildest imaginings she had never thought he would arrive like this in the middle of a working day. In truth, she had not expected to see him again, not like this, the two of them alone together. She saw him look again at the painting she was doing and felt embarrassed that he had caught her painting flowers he had sent. Does he know, she wondered? He sat next to her on the little wooden bench, his shoulder brushing against hers. She feared he had come to belatedly give her the dressing down she knew she deserved. She hung her head.

'I've been thinking things over,' he said.

She steeled herself for some home truths.

'Since I saw you last pretty much all I've been thinking about was what you told me that day.' She opened her mouth to say something and to her surprise he placed a finger against her lips. 'I reckon we were doing OK until Collins came along and stirred things up. What happens next is down to us.' He glanced at her. She didn't look up and he registered the tension in her body, not sure what to make of it. Perhaps she didn't want him there hence her discomfort. He felt like giving up but what Clarissa had said about happiness being in short supply spurred him on.

'Would it hurt for us to pretend things didn't go wrong at the ball, after all?' he said. Rose looked at him, taken aback. 'We never even got to celebrate your birthday.'

She did not dare to hope that he was really willing to put all that had gone on behind them.

'A few weeks back I thought I might lose my mother and it made me take stock. I don't want to get a few years down the line and wonder why I passed up on one of the best opportunities to come my way. I'm talking about you, Rose. You and me. Right now, I'm showing my hand; everything I have, all of it laid bare.' He spread his hands. 'Now it's up to you.'

Harry had given a great deal of thought to expanding the restaurant at Marshall Field. In a short space of time the place had established itself. Fifteen tables were simply not enough. Harry was already thinking ahead to the coming World Fair. In two years, Chicago would be thronged with people. He wanted to be prepared. Cecil Crisp had sketched some ideas for a spacious new restaurant on the top floor. He had been bold, moving away from the dark wood and ornate fittings popular at the time, instead envisaging a light and airy space with large picture windows overlooking State Street. He had drawn inspiration from a high-rise building in New York. Harry thought the plans ground-breaking and likely to appeal to a clientele already accustomed to innovation at the store.

As he made his way along the management corridor with Cecil Crisp's drawings in a folder under his arm he hummed softly to himself. Another of Lois's tunes that had burrowed its way into his head. He smiled. The doctor had been right. She was fully recovered and seemed to have even more energy than before her collapse. Harry stopped in front of an unmarked office door, took a moment to adjust the knot in his tie, and gave a knock.

'Door's open.'

Inside, Marshall Field sat behind his desk in the cramped little room. The blind was drawn, adding to the bleak atmosphere. Overhead, a lamp cast a dull yellow glow. Field was dressed in a suit and tie in more or less the same deep brown as the varnish on the door and window frame. The atmosphere was stuffy. Harry had to smile again. His employer went out of his way to keep his office space unwelcoming. 'Saves me having meetings that run any longer than they need to,' he had once told Harry. 'Surprising how no one wants to spend a lot of time in here.'

Marshall Field rose to shake his hand. 'Take a seat,' he said, indicating the hard wooden chair reserved for visitors. 'Glad to hear about Lois. Must have given you quite a start.'

'I was worried out of my mind but she's doing well, thank goodness,' Harry said, sitting down, the chair tilting to one side. He shifted position. The chair wobbled. He would keep the meeting short.

Marshall Field eyed the portfolio Harry had placed on the desk. 'Something to show me?'

Harry talked him through his idea to create a new and bigger restaurant. He showed him the drawings Cecil Crisp had done, ran through figures. 'We could be taking ten times as much if we had the capacity,' Harry said.

Field looked thoughtful. 'You're really convinced people want to dine in a store?' he said.

'I know they do. When the fair opens in two years from now the city is going to go crazy. I think we should be prepared, build up our trade well ahead, then look at staying open late to capitalize on the extra business the fair will generate.' He waited a moment. 'We're already looking at theming the windows and displays throughout the store to reflect what's going on with the fair.'

Marshall Field moved his glasses further up the bridge of his nose. 'You're not my ideas man for nothing, Harry, I'll give you that.'

Harry pushed the portfolio across the desk. 'I want every visitor who comes to Chicago for the fair to find their way to Marshall Field. I'll see to it the press give us plenty of coverage.'

Field had no doubt he would. Harry was the most skilled marketing man he had ever come across. He nodded. 'Seems you're ahead of the pack,' he said.

Harry was finding the hard chair uncomfortable. If he was to get to the matter of his partnership he had better be quick before he lost all feeling in his backside.

'I wanted to mention one more thing,' he said. 'Have you considered my proposal for a partnership?'

Marshall Field was watching him closely. His expression gave nothing away. If only the man played poker, Harry thought, he would clean up.

'You know how much I value you,' Field said. 'You've transformed the business, elevated the store to a height that, frankly, I had not considered possible. We were doing well before you got your hands on the reins, Harry, but now …' he frowned.

Harry sensed this was a preamble to letting him down, albeit gently. *You're a real asset but I don't see you as partnership material.* He was braced for disappointment.

Marshall Field kept talking, reeling off figures about turnover going up substantially in the time Harry had been in post, citing his many innovations. It was the longest speech Harry had ever heard his employer make. He moved a fraction in the uncomfortable chair as Field fixed him with an intense gaze and switched focus to a set of figures unfamiliar to Harry. It took a moment for Harry to follow. So dry was Marshall Field in his delivery, so lacking in anything that could be construed as cheer, Harry could not be sure he had entirely grasped the meaning of what was being said. He felt a tremor of excitement and leaned forward, the chair beneath him giving a perilous wobble.

'Could you say that again, sir?' he said, his heart rate becoming more rapid.

Field obliged. He was offering his ideas man a raise, a slice of the profits. Harry was to be made a partner with a stake in the future success of the store. Field kept going, explaining in fine detail how the new arrangement would work. It had taken him weeks to think things through, during which time he had considered every aspect of what he now proposed. By the time Harry got to his feet to shake on the deal he was cramping up from sitting for so long. He didn't care. A partnership. At last. As he hobbled back along the corridor he could barely contain the euphoria he felt and threw his arms around his startled secretary before asking her to put in a call to Drew Oliver at the *Herald*. 'Tell him to get over here, soon as he likes. There's good news to share,' he told her, going straight to the cabinet in his office where he kept his cigars. A flustered Mary Walters straightened her collar and did as he asked, nonplussed that a meeting with the notoriously crusty Mr Field should have sparked in Harry such exuberance.

39.

When Harry suggested dinner at the Wellington Hotel, Rose could not help wondering if it was such a good idea. The last time they had been there was for that awkward lunch when neither of them had managed to eat more than a few mouthfuls of food. Even though they had at least begun the process of clearing the air she had less than happy associations with the place. The thought of going there again, so soon, induced a mild sense of panic. In her mind, where Harry was concerned, the Wellington would be forever charged with significance. She would have preferred a restaurant with fewer overtones. There was something in the tone of Harry's note, however, that piqued at her curiosity. In the space of a few words he had managed to convey both a sense of urgency and something else; something she was not quite able to put her finger on. Celebration, perhaps. Unless she was reading too much into a short sentence about his having something to share with her that really could not wait. Whatever it was, it had to be important.

She dressed carefully, choosing a dress in a heavy purple satin that gave the appearance of changing colour as she moved, depending on the light. Not sure how to read the mood of the occasion, she kept her hair simple and decided against wearing any jewellery. It seemed appropriate.

As soon as she arrived at the restaurant she saw something different about Harry, who came to greet her and lead her to their table. It was there in his walk, which had a bounce about it. Swagger, almost. His eyes were bright, a broad smile on his face. His confidence as he bent and kissed her gloved hand was palpable. It's the Harry of old, she thought, relieved. Seeing him back at his best filled her with hope for the future.

'Something must have happened,' she said, as she sat down and removed her gloves.

Harry grinned. 'Marshall Field has made me a partner,' he said, the words coming out in a hurry.

'Harry, that's wonderful news. Congratulations.' For a moment he said nothing, simply looked at her, his smile lighting up his face. She laughed. 'I don't need to ask how you feel – it's there to see, written in your expression.'

He reached over and clasped her hand. 'Things are coming right,' he said. 'My mother is well, business could not be better-' He hesitated. 'And there's you, Rose. The two of us back on good terms. I can't tell you how happy that makes me.'

She looked away, still ashamed at what had happened between them and her part in it.

The pressure on her hand increased a fraction and she glanced up to find Harry watching her closely. 'Let's put the past behind us. I don't want any bad feeling, not between us. Life is too short,' he said, repeating the phrase that had leapt right to the top of his list of pertinent sayings.

She nodded. He had every reason to hold a grudge and have nothing more to do with her, yet here he was going out of his way to put things right. She really had never met anyone like him. And to think, she had almost ruined everything.

Harry gave her a look of concern. 'Hey, don't go all serious on me, not tonight. We're here to celebrate.'

She laughed again. His joy was contagious. She could not help but be moved by him.

There was a second reason for Harry's happiness, which was that he intended to give Rose the birthday gift that had spent the past few weeks inside the drawer of his desk at the office. He had lost count of the number of times he had slid the box from its velvet drawstring bag and examined the handcrafted jewellery he had commissioned. Several times he had considered giving it away, perhaps to his mother, but it was too bound up in Rose and he could not imagine anyone else wearing it. He had considered returning it to the workshop with instructions that it be melted down for scrap. That was when he had been convinced Rose was lost to him. Given the despair he had felt, quite what had made him hold onto the gift was a mystery. Somewhere, a flicker of hope must have lived on. He was very glad now he had decided to keep it.

'How is the painting going?' he asked.

Since he had come to the house that day, it had been going much better. 'I almost finished the flowers, the one I was busy with that day you called,' she said.

He seemed impressed. 'You must have worked fast.'

She had been painting with great energy following their talk. She smiled to herself. Everything had seemed lighter subsequently, her mood much improved. It had not escaped the notice of her mother, who called it the Harry Selfridge effect.

'I'd very much like to see it,' Harry said.

She wondered about owning up to where the arrangement of dried flowers she had painted came from in the first place but lost her nerve. He might think it a touch sentimental of her.

Despite Rose's protests that it was an extravagance, they both ordered lobster, the most expensive thing on the menu. They were celebrating, Harry reminded her. It was a special occasion. The Wellington was busy, most of the tables occupied, yet the service was attentive. The restaurant had got things pretty much just right, Harry thought. The only criticism he would make was that it was to some extent stuck in the past, traditional to the point of belonging to another time. It had the feel of one of those exclusive Chicago clubs so beloved of the city's old guard. He allowed himself a wry smile. The kind of place he had not been made welcome. He really didn't mind. He was not a man of the past. He was part of the bright new future of Chicago. When the new Marshall Field restaurant opened, it would wake up the doddery brigade so content to keep things exactly as they had always been. His restaurant would have wood-cladding, like the Wellington, but it would only cover the lower half of the walls and be painted in a soft creamy white. The ornate chandeliers would go, replaced with something more modern. Already in his mind's eye he could picture how it would look. He tucked into his lobster. One thing you could not fault the Wellington on was its food, he thought.

'Is everything OK?' he asked Rose.

'Wonderful,' she said. She glanced about her. 'Seems like this is *the* place to eat in town.'

For now it is, Harry thought. He waited until they had finished eating and the plates were taken away, asking the waiter to leave them for ten minutes or so before bringing menus for dessert.

Rose sat back in her chair and made a face. 'I'm really not sure I could eat dessert,' she said.

'Me neither but we can take a look at what they've got. We may feel like sharing something.'

She imagined a single plate between them, two spoons, and it struck her as the most intimate suggestion he had ever made.

'I have something for you,' he said. 'The gift I meant to give you at the ball once it got past twelve and the night crossed into your birthday. I didn't get a chance.' There was no reproach in his voice. 'It's a little late but I hope you like it.' He placed the velvet pouch on the table in front of her.

Rose stared at it for a moment. Her throat was dry. 'Harry, really, you didn't have to.' What she was thinking was that she did not deserve whatever it was he had got for her. Another ripple of shame and guilt went through her.

'Open it,' he said.

For several seconds she kept her eyes on the little drawstring bag. Harry had shown enormous generosity. It was her turn now to accept what he had for her with gratitude. Her mother often said it was more difficult to receive a gift and be gracious about it than it was to give. That certainly applied in this case. What had Harry said earlier about not wanting any bad feeling between them? This was her chance to let go of the past. She imagined how he must have felt at the ball, not being able to find her as midnight struck. Again, the guilt took hold of her only this time she swept it aside. She undid the drawstring and took out a small leather box, gave Harry a questioning look.

'Open it,' he said again.

She took out a necklace, a delicate rose and white gold heart, strands of the precious metal woven into a fine mesh. There was something inside. She peered at it. A tiny solid heart. She had never seen anything like it. It was exquisite.

'Harry,' she began, not trusting herself to speak.

'You like it?'

She held his gaze. 'It's perfect,' she said.

'Here, let me.' He stood up, took the necklace from her and fastened the clasp at the back of her neck. The chain was short and the hearts lay just beneath her throat. It looked exactly as he had imagined.

'There's no mirror so you're going to have to trust me on this,' he said, sitting down again. 'It looks just right.'

She reached up and touched the hearts. 'It's so unusual.'

'It's unique. I had it made for you. When I told the designer what I had in mind he got it right away. He did a great job.'

Rose was deeply moved. No one had ever shown her such consideration. She put a hand on Harry's wrist. 'It's the most beautiful thing I've ever been given,' she said. She had a new appreciation of him. It had been clear all along that Harry had an inventive mind when it came to business. Only now was she seeing that his flair went much further. He might not be an artist but she had no doubt about his ability to be creative.

'It suits you very well.'

'Thank you, Harry, I will cherish it.'

He nodded, pleased. Her hand remained on his wrist.

'How about we share a dessert?' he said.

40.

Summer was fading, the cool stirrings of autumn edging ever nearer. The change in seasons was most apparent in the mornings, Harry noticed. At six a.m. when he got up it was decidedly chilly and a roaring fire was now lit each morning in the room where he and Lois ate breakfast. Still, there were some glorious bright and balmy days as September petered out and Harry revelled in the tail end of summer. He felt wildly optimistic about the future. Becoming a partner at the store had proved invigorating. He had more energy than ever, more ideas. The coming World Fair two years along the line would invigorate Chicago and he intended to capitalize on the anticipated boost in the city's trade. His new status at Marshall Field had given him a sense of freedom in terms of the plans he was able to make. What it had also done was validate him, show everyone else what he already knew; that he had outstanding abilities. He knew he was the talk of the Chicago Club, that even those who had dismissed him and labelled him Field's office boy, were now forced to admit a grudging respect. Office boy. So, what if he was? He had proved it was possible to rise from the bottom of the heap to damned near the top. He remained as ambitious as ever and had no intention of settling for the prize he now had. In tandem with the work he was doing at the store he was also quietly drawing up plans for a new spectacular venture of his own. It was all very much inside his head but the more he thought about it the more real it became. He intended to pursue his dream of opening his own store. With each passing day, he became more convinced he had what it took to make it happen.

On the final Sunday of September the weather was glorious and Harry took Rose to Lake Park where they found shade on a bench under a towering Red Oak tree. The few slivers of sunlight that found their way through the canopy of crimson leaves gave the ground a dappled appearance. Harry felt utterly content, as if he were at the most auspicious stage of his life. He smiled inwardly. It was not something he would speak openly about, suspecting any spell of great good fortune tended to be followed by its exact opposite. Then again, the same applied in reverse, in his experience at any rate. He recognized that he was what Lois would call blessed, both professionally and personally. He stole a look at Rose, barely able to believe he had found a woman in whose company he was so at ease. Before Rose, he had doubted he would ever find someone he felt serious about; a woman he could imagine being with for the rest of his days. His involvements had always been fleeting, never serious. On some level, Harry knew he had compared each of the women in his life with Lois, inevitably coming to the conclusion they failed to measure up. Deep down, he had thought it unlikely any woman ever could.

And then came Rose.

He glanced at her again. She too seemed completely at ease. Following her gaze, he found her attention on the park's ornate cast-iron fountain with its odd-looking gargoyles. He checked his pocket watch. They were due back for tea with Lois in an hour or so. No rush.

'There's something very soothing about water,' Rose said. 'I wish I'd thought about some kind of fountain for Hyde Park.'

'You still could,' he said.

She frowned. 'I'm not sure where I would put it now.'

They fell silent again. Only one area of Harry's life was still causing him concern and it was to do with his missing father. He had not even spoken to Rose about it. It seemed too big a secret. Also, he was afraid she would take him to task for going behind Lois's back. It was remarkable how close the two of them had become in such a short time. He hated the thought of keeping something from Rose, and also from Lois, which was probably why he had shelved plans to pursue things any further for the time being. Drew Oliver still felt Harry should return to Pittsburgh, especially now his buddy Thompson was certain a man had been residing in the Charlotte Street house and still might be. The timing seemed off to Harry. He needed to square things with his mother and with Rose first, and he really did not want to leave Chicago, even for the briefest of trips. Drew had warned him against waiting too long, implying it was a mistake to assume the situation in Pittsburgh would remain unchanged.

'Wait too long and it could be too late,' Drew had said.

Harry knew he was right but it was a risk he was willing to take.

The water gushing skywards from the fountain glittered and gleamed in the sunshine. Harry imagined diamonds cascading into the air, landing at their feet, glinting on the grass. Something came to him, a thought so clear, so obvious, he felt compelled to act on it. When he took Rose's hand it felt surprisingly cool. She turned and smiled at him.

'It's such a perfect day,' she said.

'I was thinking the same.'

'There's something magical when the seasons change.' She noticed the way he was looking at her and something in his eyes sent a shiver along her spine. She reached up and touched the heart necklace. 'What's wrong, Harry?' she said.

He shook his head. 'I don't know why I didn't think of it before,' he said.

Again, she felt a tremor, sensing something momentous, afraid.

He took her hand in both of his, bent and brushed his lips against her wrist. 'I love you, Rose. I want you to be my wife. Will you marry me?'

41.

They decided to keep the news to themselves for the time being and arrange a dinner so that Lois Selfridge and Martha Buckingham could be told at the same time. It had taken all of Harry's willpower to say nothing over tea when he and Rose returned from the park that afternoon. What neither of them knew was that the moment she set eyes on them Lois had her suspicions they were betrothed. Rose had a glow about her that was unmistakeable while Harry was even more buoyant than he had been of late. Something was going on, that much was clear. Lois put two and two together but said nothing, recognizing that the couple wanted to make an announcement in their own way at a time of their choosing. Throughout tea, during which Rose ate almost nothing, she and Harry exchanged looks, delighted little coy smiles they seemed to think went undetected. Lois behaved as if nothing unusual was taking place, even though she could almost feel the air crackle with excitement. She longed to say something and prayed they would not wait too long to make their news public. All this pretence was agony.

'The fresh air seems to have done the two of you a power of good,' she said. She gave Harry a meaningful look, then shifted her gaze to Rose.

'Ma, it's the most glorious day out there,' Harry said. His voice was loud, a touch too enthusiastic to be referring to the weather.

Lois smiled.

'It is,' Rose chimed in, similarly effusive. '*Perfect.*'

Lois nodded. As far as she could tell, it was no more remarkable a day than the one before or the one before that. There had been a long and settled spell of warm, sunny weather during September. Then again, she was sure that was not what they were not talking about at all.

'I was sitting out in the back yard but I don't seem to have got the same colour in my cheeks as you've managed. You look quite *radiant*,' she told Rose, intentionally mischievous. Rose flushed. Lois kept on looking at her. 'The last days of summer can do that to you. Give you a real glow.'

Again, a meaningful look passed between Harry and Rose, confirming what Lois had surmised. She was certain she was right. *They're engaged to be married*, she thought.

When Harry had proposed marriage, Rose felt she might pass out. It was so unexpected she had struggled to get her breath. She had no idea how long she had sat on that bench under the red oak staring at him, open-mouthed for all she knew, unable to speak. She had heard people talk of how a shock had made their heads spin but it was the first time she had actually experienced the sensation for herself. She felt giddy, off balance.

All the while she fought to get her feelings under control, Harry kept a close eye on her. His expression was one of tenderness, utter sincerity. It seemed to Rose that in his eyes was an unflinching conviction that burrowed deep within her. It was this, his way of looking at her, she found so moving. He did not press her for an answer. Having spoken those few life-changing words and asked her to be his wife, he gave her all the time she needed to think and gather her composure. *Marriage.* Slowly, as if emerging from a fog, her mind began to clear. Had the same thought not crossed her mind? It had indeed, more than once, but she had refused to allow herself to dwell on the possibility. Her secret fear had been that Harry would be unable to commit to spending his life with her. Or with anyone, for that matter. His reputation was that of a confirmed bachelor whose true mistress was his work. All the while he waited, her mind picked its way through a jumble of thoughts until clarity came. Not for a moment had he taken his eyes off her. She wondered what her own expression must be telling him. Her hand lay in his. She eased it free and saw a flicker of concern in his eyes. Reaching up, she rested her hand against his cheek.

'Yes, I'll marry you, Harry,' she said, her voice breaking with emotion. 'I'll marry you.'

That night, Harry was not in the slightest bit tired and stayed up late, long after Rose had gone and Lois had retired to bed. He went out into the front yard and lit a cigar. How he was supposed to get through the next couple of days until he and Rose could share their news he really didn't know. Harry, usually so adept at putting distractions to one side, was anxious that on this occasion he would not manage it – not when he was bursting to shout his news at the top of his voice, tell the world. He laughed at the thought. It would certainly give the neighbours something to talk about. For several minutes he sat on the stone seat set against the wall at the edge of the property. The air was fresh and cool, the clear sky dotted with a sprinkling of stars. He could see no trace of the moon. At the end of the driveway he thought he detected movement. A raccoon, perhaps. He finished his cigar and sat a while longer, his mind running ahead to marrying Rose.

Beside the gated entrance to the property, a figure in shabby clothes and a cap huddled in the shadows. The boy had been tailing Harry for days, hanging about outside Marshall Field. For two nights he had slept in the stables at the back of the house. He dug a hand deep into his pocket and pulled out a battered business card, the same one given to his mother in Pittsburgh by the well-dressed gentleman from Chicago. On one side of the card was the name and details of a reporter on the *Herald* newspaper. On the reverse side, handwritten, were just three letters: HGS. The boy had not understood their significance. He had followed the newspaper man to Marshall Field and loitered at the end of the block until he saw him emerge from the store in the company of another sharply turned-out man. The boy recognized the second man at once; the same one who had done much of the talking on the doorstep of his mother's home.

He was of most interest.

The boy's detective work led him to the grand house in the well-to-do neighbourhood where, on the pretext of looking for work, he had spoken to a gardener raking up leaves in the grounds of one of the properties. The sharp-looking man he had seen in Pittsburgh turned out to be something high up in a store in town. His name was Harry Gordon Selfridge. HGS. It was this discovery that set the boy's heart racing. Now, he understood he was on the trail of something significant.

He folded the card and put it back inside his trouser pocket. His mother might have had nothing to say to the callers from Chicago about Robert Selfridge but, at fifteen, he was old enough to make up his own mind. He could not let it rest, would not, as his mother had begged him to do. He had to know about the man who had come knocking at their door.

A man named Selfridge.

From his vantage point he watched Harry put out his cigar and go indoors.

Upstairs, as Harry prepared to turn in for the night, he gave thanks for his happiness. He saw no sense in a long engagement. They should arrange the wedding as soon as was practically possible. He remembered what Danny Donovan in the packing department of Marshall Field had said about choosing November 11 as his wedding day. Eleven-eleven had a ring to it, he had said. It certainly did. Harry pondered. It was only a few weeks off, surely not long enough to arrange the kind of special day he wanted for Rose. *Come on, Harry*, he told himself. *Even in a tight corner, there's no one more able than you to make things happen.* He smiled. Their wedding day was going to be perfect, he would see to it. Nothing would get in the way of the love he felt for Rose and their future happiness. *Life is short*, he reminded himself. Why wait? He would let the past lie and stop chasing after the ghost of his father. It was the here and now that mattered. What came next would determine his happiness – not what had gone before.

In the stable block, the boy settled down for the night. There was an important connection between his father, Robert Selfridge, and this well-to-do gentleman, that much he knew. Now he intended to make it his business to uncover the truth.

Acknowledgments

Sincere thanks to the following:

Kristen Harrison and Nerys Hudson at The Curved House. Emma King, whose cover design was just right.

Jason Anderson and Marina Anderson at Polgarus Studio.

Heather Hill and Janet O'Kane, who generously gave advice. Helen Barbour, Chris Hill, Michael Moran, Jennifer Tracey and Rowan Whiteside for reading, reviewing and tweeting.

June Taylor. For encouragement.

Pauleen McNestrie. For believing.

My love and thanks to Mick Miller. For everything.

About the Author

Maria Malone is a non-fiction author with a passion for television. A former broadcast journalist, she has worked as a producer in factual and entertainment programming and has filmed behind-the-scenes on *Poirot, Prime Suspect, Henry VIII* and many other UK dramas. She was on the set of *Mr Selfridge* during Season 2, filming a bonus feature for the series DVD, and interviewed Jeremy Piven, Frances O'Connor and the rest of the cast. So inspired was she by the characters of Harry and Rose, and their enduring love story, it set her thinking about what might have made the two of them click when they first met in Chicago before coming to London … The result is *When Harry Met Rose: Mr Selfridge and the Search for Love.*

Maria's other books include *The Tube Exposed, Popstars*, and *The Frog Princess*. She is also a ghostwriter of autobiographies.

Also available, the second novel in the Harry Selfridge series, *Marriage, Misunderstanding and Mr Selfridge*

Maria loves to hear from readers and can be contacted at
whenharrymetrose@gmail.com
www.mariamalonebooks.com
On twitter **@mariasmalone**
Also see Maria Malone's Amazon page

52386696R00133

Made in the USA
Lexington, KY
27 May 2016